ILLUSTRATED · COMPLETE

Tevye the Dairyman

ILLUSTRATOR'S FOREWORD

When the publisher, Joseph Simon, asked me to illustrate the Tevye the Dairyman *stories, I became very interested because it took me back to my youth, when my father would read the stories in the original Yiddish to our mother and ten of us children. Eventually, I read the stories in English translation. They inspired me to convert Sholem-Aleykhem's word pictures into graphic form, so that the reader would see what I saw. The more of his writings that I read, the more I wanted to illustrate them.*

Sholem-Aleykhem wrote for the everyday Yiddish reader, trying to have him see the irony and humor of life in "The Old Country." A life that, for Jews, was often unhappy and poor, as well as frustrated at the burdens imposed on them by an hostile Czarist regime.

Even though this is not a coloring book, the illustrations are done to complement the stories. But if you, or your family, get a desire to color them, then feel free to do so, and let your imagination take you into the world of Tevye the Dairyman.

MANUEL BENNETT

SHOLEM-ALEYKHEM'S

Tevye the Dairyman

COMPLETE • ILLUSTRATED

ILLUSTRATED BY MANUEL BENNETT

Joseph Simon / Pangloss Press

MALIBU, CALIFORNIA

This edition Copyright 1994
by Pangloss Press
Illustrations by Manuel Bennett
Design by Joseph Simon

Library of Congress Cataloging-in-Publication Data

Sholem-Aleykhem, 1859-1916.
  [Tevye der milkhiker. English]
  Sholem-Aleykhem's Tevye the dairyman : complete : illustrated /
Sholem-Aleykhem : illustrated by Manuel Bennett.
    p. cm.
  Translated by Miriam Katz.
  ISBN 0-934710-31-7 : $12.95
    I. Bennett, Manuel, 1921-   . II. Katz, Miriam. III. Title.
IV. Title: Tevye the dairyman.
PJ5129.R2T4513   1994
839'.0133—dc20   94-9304
                                                                   CIP

Contents

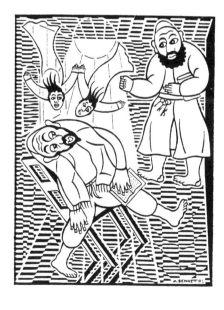

"I bought you a cow then for fifty rubles, it would have been a steal at fifty-five. What if it did drop dead three days later? It was not my fault: didn't the other cow I bought you also kick the bucket?"

I Am Not Worthy

With all respect to my very dear friend Reb Sholom Aleichem, God grant you health and a good living together with your wife and children, let great pleasure be yours wherever you go, amen!

"I am not worthy!" So I must say using the words our forefather Jacob said—in the Sabbath section of the Torah—when he set out against Esau, begging your pardon... If this is not quite right, I beg you, Mr. Sholom Aleichem, not to hold it against me, I am a simple man. You, of course, know more than I do—that goes without saying. Alas, a person coarsens in a village: who has time to look into a book or learn a portion of the Torah with Rashi's commentaries, or anything else? It's a lucky thing that when summer arrives the rich people from Yehupetz come to Boiberik to their summer homes, their *dachas,* so that one is likely to meet an enlightened person sometimes, to hear a good word. Believe me, the remembrance of those days when you sat near me in the woods listening to my foolish yarns is dearer to my heart than any amount of money! I don't understand how I found so much favor in your eyes that you should take up with such an insignificant person and even write letters to me and, above all, put my name into a book, serve me to the world as a dainty dish, just as if I were I don't know who, so I may well say: *"I am not worthy!"* True, I am really a good friend of yours, let God help me to a hundredth part of what I wish you! You saw, I am sure, how well I served you back in the good old days when you lived in the big *dacha*—do you remember? I bought you a cow then for fifty rubles, it would have been a steal at fifty-five. What if it did drop dead three days later? It was not my fault at all: didn't the other cow I gave you also kick the bucket? You know very well yourself how hard I took this, I absolutely lost my head then! I tried my very hardest to get you the best of everything, so help me God, and you, too, if he so wills, in the coming year. He should, as they say, *"make our days the same as in olden times."* And let God help me make a living and be

healthy, and my horse—begging your pardon—should be healthy, and my cows should give enough milk for me to go on serving you with my cheese and butter in the best possible manner, you and all the rich people from Yehupetz, God grant them success in their undertakings, all good things and happiness. And the same to you for the trouble you take, for bothering yourself on my account, for the honor you are paying me with your book, I can only repeat: *"I am not worthy!"* With what have I earned such an honor—that a world of people should suddenly become aware that on the other side of Boiberik, near Anatovka, there lives a Jew named Tevye the Dairyman? But you probably know what you are doing, I don't have to teach you wisdom, you know how to write, and in all other matters I trust your noble nature and am sure that you will see to it in Yehupetz that this book brings me, too, some benefit. It really would come in handy now: the Lord be willing, we shall soon have to think of a match for a daughter, and if He grants, maybe even for two daughters at once. Meanwhile remain in good health and be happy always, as your friend Tevye wishes you from the bottom of his heart.

Tevye

Oh, Yes! I almost forgot! When the book is ready and you are prepared to send me some money, please send it to Anatovka, care of the local slaughterer. I observe two memorial days there, one in the autumn, just before the Russian *Pokrov,* and the other around the Russian New Year. These days I spend in the *shtetl.* Ordinary letters you may send directly to me in Boiberik, addressing them: *Peredat gospodinu Tevelu molochnaho yevrei*.*

1895

---

*To be forwarded to Mister Tevel the milky Jew (incorrect Russian).—*Tr.*

The Grand Prize

A wonderful narrative describing how Tevye the Dairyman, a poor man burdened with a large family, was suddenly, out of the blue, made happy through a miraculous event worthy of being written up in a book. It is presented as told by Tevye himself, word for word .

> "Who raiseth up the poor out of the dust, And lifteth up the needy out of the dunghill..."
> Psalms, 113:7

If you are destined to win a grand prize, Mr. Sholom Aleichem, it comes right home to you. As it is said in the Psalms, when it moves your way it comes in a rush! Cleverness or skill have nothing to do with it. But if, God forbid, it goes the other way—you may talk yourself blue in the face and it will be of as much use as last winter's snow Over a bad horse, they say, neither wisdom nor advice can prevail. A man toils, struggles, gets so exhausted he is ready to lay himself down and die! Then all of a sudden, no one knows from what and from where, luck descends on him from all sides. As the Torah says, *"Relief and deliverance will come to the Jews."* It means that while his soul is still in his body, while the blood still pulses through his veins, a Jew should never lose hope. From my own experience I know how the Almighty led me to my present livelihood. How did it happen that I started selling cheese and butter all of a sudden, when my grandmother's granny never dealt in dairy foods? It will be worth your while to hear the whole story from beginning to end. I'll sit down here next to you on the grass and let my horse graze meanwhile, for, as it is said, *"the soul of everything that lives"*—a horse is also one of God's creatures.

Well, it was around *Shabuoth* time—I don't want to tell any lies, it might have been a week or two before *Shabuoth,* or maybe even a few weeks after. Don't forget that little by little, to be precise, a year of Sundays has already gone by since then, that is, exactly nine years or ten, or maybe a bit more.

In those days I was not the same person I am now. That is, I was the same Tevye, but different. As they say, the same old woman but under a different veil. I was then—may this never happen to you—as poor as poor can be, although, to tell the truth, I am by far no rich man today. You and I together should this summer earn what I would need to be as rich as Brodsky, but as compared to those days I am today a well-to-do man with my own horse and wagon, with a couple of, knock on wood, milch cows and another cow that is due to calve any day now. It would be a sin to complain, we have cheese and butter and fresh cream every day, all earned with our own labor, we all work, nobody is idle. My wife, bless her, milks the cows, the children carry the jugs and churn the butter, while I myself, as you see, drive to the market early every morning and call at every Boiberik *dacha*. I get to meet this person, that person, all the important people from Yehupetz, I chat a while with them and this makes me feel that I am also worth something in the world, that I am, as they say, no "lame tailor". To say nothing of the Sabbath; I'm really a king then, I look into a Jewish book, I read the weekly portion of the Torah, a bit of *Targum*, some of the Psalms, *Perek*, this, that, and something else; looking at me, Mr. Sholom Aleichem, you probably think: "Eh, this Tevye really amounts to something!.."

But what was it I began to tell you? Oh, yes, so at that time, I was, with God's help, a bitterly poor man, starving to death—such a fate shouldn't befall others—with my wife and children three times a day not counting supper. I toiled like a mule, hauling logs from the woods to load into box-cars at the railway station for, it's a disgrace to say, two *zlotys** a day, and this not every day, either. Go and support such a houseful of eaters, God bless them, and also, begging your pardon, my boarder, the horse, who wanted to know nothing of Rashi's commentaries but had to munch fodder every day without any excuse at all!

So what does God do? It is He, after all, who feeds and nurtures us, He rules this little world in a wise and orderly manner. Seeing how I struggle for a piece of bread, He says to me: "You think, Tevye, that it's already the end of the world, that the sky has

---

*A Polish monetary unit equivalent to less than half of a U.S. dollar.—*Tr.*

fallen down on you? Pooh, you are a big fool! Just wait, you'll see how, when God so wills, your luck will about-face and a bright light will shine in all the nooks and crannies." Like in the High Holiday hymn describing the Day of Judgment: *"Who will be raised and who flung down"*—who will ride and who go on foot. The principle of this is faith—a Jew must hope, only hope and have confidence. What if you do suffer meanwhile? After all, that is why we are Jews, as it is written: *"Thou hast chosen us"* — it is not for nothing that the whole world is envious of us. Why am I telling you this? I am telling you what God did for me, really *"miracles and wonders,"* you must hear it.

"And there came the day." One summer evening I was driving my empty wagon home through the woods. My head was bowed, my heart was heavy. The horse, poor thing, could barely move its legs. "Crawl, *shlimazl,* get lost together with me! Since you are Tevye's excuse for a horse you must know what it means to fast all of a long summer day!" There was silence all around me, every crack of my whip echoed and re-echoed in the woods. The sun was setting, the day was dying. The shadows of the trees became longer and longer—as long as the Jewish exile. As the dusk thickened, a great gloom settled in my heart. Various thoughts flitted through my mind, images of people long dead came towards me. Then I remembered my home, woe is me! The house is dark and bleak, the children, bless them, are naked and barefoot, waiting, poor things, for their *Tateh,* their father the *shlimazl,* hoping he will bring them a fresh loaf of bread or maybe even a white roll. And she, my old woman, is grumbling, as women are wont to do: "Children I had to bear him, a whole seven, take and throw them—God shouldn't punish me for my words—alive into the river!" Nice hearing such words, eh? A man is no more than flesh and blood—the stomach cannot be filled with words. You snatch a bite of herring and then you yearn for tea, but with tea you must have sugar, and sugar, they say, is in Brodsky's refineries. "For the piece of bread I go without," says my wife, God bless her, "my innards will excuse me, but without a glass of tea in the morning I am a dead woman—the baby sucks all the juices out of me the whole night long!"

Meantime, one is, after all, something of a Jew; *Minhah,* the afternoon prayer, is no goat, it won't run away, but pray one must. Then just imagine what kind of praying it was then, just as I stood up to say *Shmin-esra,* the horse, as bad luck would have it, bolted and I had to run after the wagon, holding on to the reins and chanting: *"God of Abraham, God of Isaac, God of Jacob"*—truly a fine way to chant *Shmin-esra!* And to make it worse, I was then just in the right mood to pray with zest, from the bottom of my heart, hoping that it might, perhaps, lift the load from my soul.

Well, to make a long story short, here I was running along behind the wagon and chanting *Shmin-esra* loudly, as if I were in the cantor's pulpit in the synagogue: *"Thou sustaineth the living with loving kindness,"* and *"keeping Thy covenant even with those who sleep in the earth."* Oh, thought I, not only the dead lie in the dust... Oh, how we suffer! Not, of course, those rich people from Yehupetz who spend a whole summer at their *dachas* in Boiberik, eating and drinking and basking in luxury. Oh, God Almighty, what have I done to merit this kind of life? Am I worse than other people? Help, dear God! *"Look upon our afflictions"*—just look upon us how we toil, put an end to the wrong suffered by the wretched poor, for who, if not You, will take care of us? *"Heal us, O Lord"*—send us the medicines, the ailments we already have. *"Bless us"*—bless this year for us, O Lord our God, with every kind of crop, with corn and wheat and barley; although, thinking it over, what will I, *shlimazl* that I am, get out of it? What difference does it make to my nag—begging your pardon—whether oats are dear or cheap? But shame on me, you don't question God, and a Jew, especially, must take everything as being for his good and say: *"And this, too, is for the best"*—probably God wills it so...

"And for slanderers let there be no hope"—I went on chanting; the slanderers and the 'ristocrats who say there is no God in the world will be put to shame when they get *there*. They'll pay for their blasphemy, and with interest, because He is one who *"breaketh His enemies"*—a good payer, with Him you play no games, with Him you are humble, you implore him, you cry out to Him: *"Merciful Father"*, dear, kind Father! *"Hear our voices"*— listen to us. *"Have mercy upon us"*, have pity on my wife and children, they, poor things, are hungry! *"Deign Thou..."*—have compassion for your beloved Children of Israel, as you once did in the Holy Temple, when the Priests and the Levites... Just then— stop! The horse suddenly stopped and stood stock-still. Hastily I rolled off the last piece of *Shminesra* and then raised my eyes: two very strange creatures were coming towards me out of the forest. They were either disguised, or strangely dressed.

Bandits—flashed through my mind, but I immediately thought

better of that. Pooh, Tevye, aren't you a fool? Just reflect, you've been driving through this forest for so many years, both in the daytime and at night, why should you suddenly think of bandits today? "Giddy-up!" I shouted to my horse, took heart and treated it to a few lashes of the whip, making believe I hadn't noticed anything.

"Reb Jew, my good man, listen!" cried one of the creatures in a female voice, beckoning to me with a kerchief. "Do please stop for a moment, wait a while, don't run away, we won't do you any harm!"

Oho, an evil spirit! was my thought, but I soon told myself: You ass! Why all of a sudden devils and demons?

So I stopped the horse. Now I took a good look at the creature: females, the older one wearing a silken kerchief over her head, the younger one wearing a wig*. Their faces were flaming red and covered with beads of sweat.

"Good evening, well met!" said I very loudly, trying to look cheerful. "What do you wish? If you want to buy something I have nothing but a bellyache I wish on all my enemies, a weekful of heart pains, a head dizzy from worries, dry aches and wet anguish, troubles and misery wholesale and retail!"

"Shush, shush," they cried. "Just see how his tongue has loosened! When you hook a Jew with one word beware of your life! We don't want to buy anything at all, we only wanted to ask you whether you know the way to Boiberik?"

"To Boiberik," I exclaimed, forcing myself to laugh, "it's just as if you'd asked me whether I knew that my name was Tevye."

"Oh, so your name is Tevye? A good evening to you, Reb Tevye! We can't see what's so funny? We're strangers, from Yehupetz, we live on a *dacha* in Boiberik," they said. "We went out for a short walk early this morning, but lost our way in the woods, and have been wandering around in circles ever since and couldn't find the right way. We heard someone singing, so at first we thought, God forbid, it was a bandit. But when we got closer and saw that you were, thank God, a Jew, our hearts felt a little lighter. Now you understand?"

"Ha-ha-ha! A fine bandit!" said I, "Did you ever hear the story of the Jewish highwayman who attacked a passer-by and asked him for a pinch of snuff? If you wish I can tell it to you."

---

*Orthodox married women wear wigs.—*Tr.*

13

"Two very strange creatures were coming towards me out of the forest."

"The story leave for another time," they said. "Better show us the way to Boiberik."

"To Boiberik," I repeated. "Why, this is the right way. Even if you don't want it to, this road will take you directly into Boiberik."

"So why didn't you say so at once, why the silence?"

"Should I have shouted, or what?"

"In that case," they said, "you know, perhaps, how far it is to Boiberik?"

"It's not far," I answered, "only a few versts*, that is, something like five, six or seven, and maybe even all of eight versts."

"Eight versts!" exclaimed both women at once, wringing their hands and almost weeping. "Do you realize what you are saying? It's no trifle—eight versts!"

"Well," said I, "what can I do about it? If it were in my power I'd have made the distance a little shorter. A person must try everything in the world. On the road it happens that you have to crawl uphill through mud, and it is the Sabbath eve, to boot, the rain is lashing your face, your hands are numb with cold, your heart is faint with hunger, and—cr-ra-ash! An axle breaks."

"You're talking like a ninny," they said to me, "you are out of your mind! Telling us old wives' tales, stories from the *Arabian Nights?* We haven't the strength to take another step. Except for a glass of coffee and a butter roll, we haven't had a morsel of food all day, and here you come along with your yarns!"

"Oh, if that's the case," said I, "then it's another thing. As they say, you don't dance before you eat. The taste of hunger I understand very well, you don't have to explain... I probably haven't as much as seen any coffee or butter rolls for well over a year." As I spoke, a glass of steaming coffee with milk and a fresh butter roll appeared before my mind's eye, and other goodies, too. Oh, you *shlimazl,* I thought to myself, so you have actually been raised on coffee and butter rolls? A hunk of bread with a piece of herring isn't good enough for you? But the Tempter, Heaven preserve us, spites me with visions of coffee and of rolls! I smell coffee and taste a butter roll, fresh, delicious, soul-enlivening!

"You know what, Reb Tevye?" said the women. "It would be a good idea, since we are standing here, for us to climb into your wagon and for you to take the trouble to drive us home to Boiberik. What do you think of that?"

*An old Russian unit of linear measure equal to 3,500 ft.; 8 versts is 5.5 miles.— *TR.*

15

"A fine notion," said I, "here I'm coming *from* Boiberik while you have to go *to* Boiberik! So what's the solution?"

"Well, so what," they said, "don't you know what to do? A wise man would turn his wagon around and drive back to Boiberik. Don't worry, Reb Tevye, rest assured that when, God willing, you get us home safely we should have as many afflictions as what you'll lose on this transaction."

They're speaking gibberish to me, thought I, obscure language, most unusual! Into my head came corpses, witches, pranksters, evil spirits. You blockhead, son of a woodpecker, I told myself, why are you standing there like a stump? Jump onto your wagon, show your horse the whip and make yourself scarce! Meanwhile, however, in spite of myself, I unintentionally let out:

"Get into the wagon!"

The women didn't have to be asked twice. They climbed in, I seated myself on the box, about-faced the shafts and gave my horse a taste of the whip—one, two, three, giddy-up! But who, what, where? The animal wouldn't budge, go and cut it in two!

Well, I thought, now I understand what kind of women these are. It was no good wind that drove me to stop all of a sudden and be drawn into a conversation with women!

You must understand: on the one hand, there was the forest with its silence and gloom, on the other, these two creatures in the guise of women... My imagination ran wild. I recalled the story told about a carter who was once driving all alone through a forest. He suddenly saw a bag of oats lying in the road. He jumped off his dray and lifted the bag—it was so heavy that he all but ruptured himself before he managed to heave it onto the dray. Then he continued on his way. After a verst or so he took a look at the bag of oats—no bag, no oats. Instead there was a goat in his dray, a bearded goat. He tried to touch it but the creature stuck out a tongue a yard long, let out an eery, mad peal of laughter and vanished into thin air!

"Why aren't we moving?" asked the women.

"Why we aren't moving? You see, don't you," said I, "that the horse is not in the mood."

"So use your whip—you have one, haven't you?"

"Thanks a lot for the advice, it's a good thing you reminded me, but the trouble is that this animal has no fear of such things. He is as used to the whip as I am to poverty," said I, trying to joke, but meanwhile shaking as if in a fever.

16

To make a long story short, I poured out the bitterness of my heart on the poor beast until, with God's help, it bestirred itself *"and they went out of Refidim"*—we drove away along the road through the forest. A new thought entered my head as we jogged along: Oh, Tevye, are you an ass! *"If thou hast begun to fall"*—a pauper you were and a pauper you'll stay! Look, God has sent you an encounter that happens once in a hundred years, so why don't you settle beforehand on a payment for your services? You should know what they will give you. According to justice, conscience, humaneness, law and I don't know what else there is no sin in earning something out of such an affair. Really, why not get a lick of a bone since it has come your way? Stop your horse, you ox, and tell them, so and so, *"I will serve thee for Rachel thy daughter"*—if I receive such and such a sum from you, well and good, if not— I must ask you, begging your pardon, to get off my wagon! But then I thought again: You really are an ox, Tevye! Don't you know that a bearskin can't be sold in the forest, or, as the peasant says: *Sche nye poimav a vzhe skube,* that is, you haven't caught it yet and are already skinning it!

"Why don't we move a little faster?" asked the women, poking my back.

"What's your great hurry? Nothing good ever comes of haste," I answered, glancing at my passengers out of the corner of an eye: women, seemingly, ordinary women, one with a silken kerchief on her head, the other with a wig. They sat there looking at each other and whispering.

"Have we still far to go?" they asked.

"Most certainly no farther than from here," I answered. "Soon we'll go downhill, then uphill; after that downhill and uphill again, and only after that will come the big uphill stretch and then the road will take us right into Boiberik..."

"A piece of *shlimazl!*" said one women to the other.

"A lingering ailment," remarked the other one.

"The last straw!" exclaimed the first one.

"Looks crazy to me!" rejoined the second one.

Of course I must be crazy, thought I, since I let myself be hoodwinked!

"Where, for instance, my dear ladies, would you like to be dropped off?" I asked.

"What do you mean—dropped off?"

"It's just an expression drivers use," I answered. "In our lingo it means, 'Where do you wish me to take you when we get to Boiberik, God willing, in good health,' as people say, it's better to ask twice than to blunder once."

"Oh, so that's what you mean? Then please drive us to the green *dacha* that stands by the river on the other side of the forest. Do you know where it is?"

"Why shouldn't I know," said I, "I'm at home in Boiberik. I should have as many thousand rubles as the number of logs I've hauled to that *dacha*. Only last summer I delivered two loads of wood there at once. A rich man lived there, a millionaire from Yehupetz who must be worth at least a hundred thousand rubles, or even two hundred thousand!"

"He lives there this year, too," said the women, whispering to each other and tittering.

"Oh, so it is likely that you are some kin of his?" I asked. "Then it might not be a bad idea if you would kindly take the trouble to put in a good word for me, do me a good turn—there might be something for me to do, some kind of a job. I know a young man, Israel is his name, he lived near our *shtetl...* he was just a nobody. Well, now he's gone up high, nobody knows how, he's become a big shot, earns twenty rubles a week, or even forty— I don't know! Some people have luck! Or, for instance, what does our *shokhet's* son-in-law lack? What would have happened to him if he hadn't gone away to Yehupetz? True, he did have a real hard time during the first few years, he almost starved to death. But his troubles are over now—the same should happen to me. He sends money home already and wants to bring over his wife and children, but he has no residence permit*. So how come *he* lives there? He has plenty of troubles, I can tell you that... Well, I always say that if you live long enough you are bound to get somewhere. Here is the river, and here is the big *dacha!*" With these words I drove dashingly right up to the porch.

Our appearance cause a great uproar! What joyous exclamations and questions!

"Oh, oh, Granny!" "Mother!" "Auntie!" "Our lost ones have returned!" "Congratulations!" "But where were you?" "A whole day, we were worried sick!" "We sent post-riders in all directions."

---

*In tsarist Russia Jews had to live within the Pale of Settlement in small towns. Special residence permits were needed for living in larger towns and cities—*Tr.*

"We thought, who knows what might have happened. Wolves, or maybe bandits, God forbid!" "So what's the story?"

"It's a fine story, really: we got lost in the woods and wandered far away, ten versts maybe. Suddenly there appeared a Jew. What kind of Jew?... A *shlimazl*, with a horse and wagon... Had trouble persuading him."

"Of all the horrible nightmares! All alone, with no guide?" "What an adventure, what an ordeal! We must say a prayer for deliverance from danger!"

Soon lamps were brought out to the porch, the table was set, and they began to bring out hot samovars, tea-glasses, sugar, preserves, dainty pastries, fresh-smelling butter rolls, followed by all kinds of food, the most expensive sorts, broths twinkling with fat, roasts and goose, the best wines and cordials.

I stood outside, observing from a distance how, knock on wood, these Yehupetz rich folk ate and drank, no harm should befall them. It's worth pawning your last shirt, I thought, only to become a rich man! What fell to the ground from this table would be enough, I thought, to last my children a whole week until Saturday. Oh, kind, true God, You are a long-bearing Lord, a great God and a good God, merciful and just, why is it that You give one everything, the other nothing? One has butter-rolls, the other—the plagues of Egypt. Then I had another thought: Eh, but you are a great fool, Tevye, upon my word. Do you want to tell *Him* how to rule the world? Since *He* wills it so, then so it must be; if it had to be otherwise, it would have been otherwise. But why shouldn't things actually be otherwise? The answer is: *"We were slaves..."* That's why we are Jews, the Chosen Ones of this world. A Jew must live with faith and confidence; he must believe, firstly, that there is a God in the world, and he must trust in the Eternal One, trust that, God willing, things will get better.

"Where is that man?" I heard somebody ask. "Has he already left, the *shlimazl?*"

"God forbid!" I raised my voice from the distance. "How could I leave without saying goodbye? *Sholom aleichem,* a good evening to you, *'God bless the sitters,'* eat in good health, and welcome!"

"Come over here, why are you standing out there in the dark," they said. "Let us at least have a look at you, see your face. Perhaps you'll take a drop of vodka?"

"A drop of vodka? Ah," said I, "who refuses to take a drop of

"The table was set, and they began to bring out hot samovars, tea-glasses, sugar, preserves…roasts and goose, the best wines and cordials."

vodka? As the Good Book says: *'What is for health and what is for death,'* which means, as Rashi explains, that God is God and vodka is vodka. *Lehayim!"* said I and emptied the glass. "May God keep you wealthy and happy. Jews should always be Jews, God should grant them health and strength to endure their troubles."

"What is your name?" asked the rich man, the *gvir* himself, a fine-looking man wearing a skullcap. "Where do you come from, where do you live, how do you make a living? Are you married? Do you have any children and how many?"

"Children? It would be a sin to complain," said I, "for if each one of them is worth a million, as my Golda wants to convince me, then I'm richer than the richest man in Yehupetz. The trouble is that poor is not rich, crooked is not straight, as the Book says: *'Who has made a distinction between the sacred and the profane,'* meaning that he is merry who has the *mezumen*. However, it is the Brodskys who have the money, while I have daughters. And from girls, as they say, the head twirls. But no matter, God is our Father. He rules, that is, He sits up above and we struggle down below. One toils, hauls wood—what else is there to do? As the *Gemara* says: 'If you can't have a meat dish then a herring is a good fish.' The whole trouble is the eating. As my grandmother, God rest her soul, used to say: 'If the mouth weren't so bold, the head would be crowned with gold.' Please excuse me, but there is nothing straighter than a crooked ladder and nothing crookeder than a straight word, especially when you down some vodka on an empty stomach."

"Let the man have something to eat!" ordered the *gvir*, and at once there appeared on the table all kinds of food: fish and meat, roasts, quarters of fowls, and no end of gizzards and livers.

"Will you have something to eat?" they asked. "Then go wash your hands."

"A sick man you ask, a healthy one you give," I said. "But thank you anyhow. A drop of vodka—that's all right, but to sit down to such a feast while out there, at home, my wife and children, God bless them... If it were your kind will to..."

In short, they must have understood what I meant, for they began to load my wagon, each one carrying something separately: this one a white loaf, that one some fish, another one a roast, this one a quarter of a fowl, that one tea and sugar, a third one a pot of drawn fat, a fourth—a jar of jam.

"These things," they told me "you'll take home as a gift to

your wife and children. Now tell us what we should pay you for the trouble you took on our account."

"What an idea—I should tell you! As much as your kind nature wills, that much you will pay me. We won't haggle," I said, "a gold piece less, a gold piece more, as they say. A pauper can't become any poorer."

"No, we want to hear from you yourself, Reb Tevye! Don't be afraid," they said, "for this, God forbid, we won't chop your head off."

What does one do in such a case, I thought. It's a plight: if I say "a ruble" when perhaps they might give me two!.. If I say "two rubles" I'm afraid they might look at me as if I were crazy: what is there to pay two rubles for?

But at this point my tongue slipped, and before I knew it I cried out: "A trey!!!"

This made the whole company laugh so loudly that I thought the earth would swallow me.

"Please excuse me if I've said the wrong thing," I said. "A horse goes on four legs and sometimes stumbles, so what can you expect of a man with one tongue?"

The merriment went up a pitch, they actually held their sides with laughter.

"Let there be an end to your laughter!" cried the *gvir* and took a big purse out of his inner pocket, and from the purse he pulled out—how much do you think? A tenner, a note as red as fire, I'm telling you the truth, as both of us live and breathe! And then he said:

"This you have from me, and you, children, give from your pockets as much as you think you should."

In short, what can I say? Five-ruble, three-ruble and one ruble notes began to fly onto the table. My limbs trembled so that I thought I'd faint.

"Well, what are you standing there for?" asked the *gvir.* "Take up the few rubles from the table and go home in good health to your wife and children."

"God bless you," said I, "and reward you many times over, you should have tenfold, a hundredfold as much as you have, and all good things and great happiness!" With these words I raked up the money with both hands, without counting, and crammed it into all my pockets.

"Good night," I said, "a good future and good health to you, and great happiness to you and your children and your children's children."

As I turned to go to my wagon the *gvirte,* the rich man's wife, she of the silken kerchief, called me back:

"Wait a moment, Reb Tevye. From me you shall receive a special gift if, God willing, you come here tomorrow morning. I have a dun-colored cow, it used to be a wonderful milker, gave twenty-four glasses of milk. Somebody cast a 'good' eye on it and now it no longer milks—that is, you can milk it, but no milk comes out..."

"A long life to you," said I, "don't trouble yourself, with us your cow will both be milked and give milk. My old woman, God bless her, is so clever that she shreds noodles from nothing, with five fingers makes gruel, celebrates the Sabbath out of miracles and puts the children to bed with slaps... Don't be angry with me, please excuse me, I beg your pardon, perhaps I let my tongue run away with me. A good night, health and joy be yours forever." With these words I went out into the yard.

I looked for my horse—woe is me, a misfortune, a calamity! I searched here and there and everywhere— *"the child is not,"* there is no horse!

Well, Tevye, I thought to myself, you've been had!

And then there came to my mind a fine story I once read in a book: a company of "evil brethren" once caught an honest Jew, a Hasid, when he was away from home, and lured him to an out-of-the-way palace where they wined him and dined him. Suddenly they all disappeared, and he was left all alone with a female who soon turned into a wild beast that quickly became a cat, and the cat—a dragon. Look out, Tevye, I said to myself, maybe you are being duped?!

"Why are you fumbling out there, what are you grumbling about?" somebody asked me.

"Why am I fumbling!? Woe is me that I live in this world," I answered, "my horse is gone."

"Your horse," they answered, "is in the stable, just take the trouble to go over there, into the stable."

I went into the stable, and what did I see? Yes, truly, as I am a Jew! My nag was faring quite well, standing among the *gvir's* horses, its jaws immersed in oats, chewing with great gusto!

23

"Listen here, my sage," I said to the horse, "it's time we went home. One shouldn't go for food so greedily. An extra bite may cause great harm."

In short, I finally managed to talk the horse, begging your pardon, into letting me harness it, and then I set out for home in a lively, merry mood, chanting *"Almighty Lord"* as if I were tipsy. The horse, too, had undergone a great change, had grown, as it were, a new skin. It no longer waited for a lash from the whip, it ran as smoothly as a psalm.

It was a bit latish when we got home, but I woke up my wife with a happy shout.

"Happy holiday, *mazl-tov,* congratulations, Golda!"

"A black and desolate *mazl-tov* to you," she answered. "what's put you into such a festive humor, my dear bread-winner? Are you returning from a wedding or a circumcision celebration, my gold-spinner?

"A wedding and a circumcision rolled into one! Just you wait, my wife, I'll show you a treasure," said I, "but first wake up the children, let them, poor things, also partake of the Yehupetz dainties."

"Either you are insane, crazy or deranged, or out of your mind. You talk like a madman, God have mercy on us!" So spoke my wife and dealt me out the whole chapter of curses as a woman usually does.

"A woman," said I, "is always a woman. It was not for nothing that King Solomon said that among his thousand wives he couldn't find a single level-headed one. It is indeed a lucky thing, upon my word, that it is no longer the fashion to have a lot of wives," and I went outside to my wagon and brought in and put out on the table all the goodies that had been packed up for me.

When my crew saw the loaves and rolls, when they caught a sniff of the meat, they pounced on the food like a pack of hungry wolves, poor things. Their hands trembled as they snatched the food, but their jaws worked unerringly. As the Book says: *"And they did eat"*—and Rashi explains: they crackled like locusts. Tears came to my eyes.

"So tell us," said my spouse, "who gave a meal for the poor, or was it just a feast, and why are you so proud of yourself?"

"Have patience, Golda, you'll learn everything in good time. But first blow up the samovar, then we'll all sit down around the table and drink tea in proper style. A man lives only once, not

24

twice, especially now when we already have a cow of our own that gives twenty-four glasses of milk; tomorrow, God willing, I'll bring the cow home. Now, Golda," said I, pulling out the whole pack of money, "try and guess how much money we have here!"

I took a look at my wife—she was as pale as death, couldn't utter a word.

"God be with you, Golda darling," I exclaimed, "what's scared you so? Maybe you are afraid that I stole this money or held up someone? You ought to be ashamed of yourself! You've been Tevye's wife for such a long time, how can you think such things? You little fool, this is *kosher* money, earned honestly by my own wit and toil. I saved two souls from great danger, if not for me, God knows that would have happened to them!"

In short, I told her the whole story from beginning to end: how God had led me by the hand. After that we both began to count the money over and over—it was exactly twice eighteen* and one extra, so there we had a bundle of thirty-seven rubles! My wife burst into tears.

"Why are you crying, silly woman?" I asked.

"How should I not cry when the tears flow?" she answered. "When the heart is full the eyes overflow. So help me God—my heart told me that you would return with good tidings. I can't remember when Grandmother Tzeitl, may she rest in peace, last appeared to me in a dream. I was lying asleep and suddenly I dreamed I saw a brimful pail of milk. Grandmother Tzeitl was carrying this pail, covered with her apron to shield it from the evil eye, and the children were wailing, 'Mama, a sip of mi-i-ilk!'"

"Don't gobble up the noodles before the Sabbath, dear heart," said I, "let Grandmother Tzeitl abide in bright paradise, I don't know whether we'll be the richer for that. However, if God could perform the miracle that brought us a cow, He will probably see to it that the cow is a real cow... Let us better put our heads together, Golda my heart, and decide what to do with the money."

"By all means," said Golda, "what do you plan to do with so much, knock on wood, money?"

"With the greatest pleasure," said I. "But what do *you* think we might do with such a big, knock on wood, sum?"

So when we both began to think, to plan, to rack our brains, to consider all kinds of businesses. What didn't we buy and sell

---

*Eighteen—a good-luck number . —*Tr.*

25

that night! We bought a pair of horses and soon sold them at a profit; we opened a grocery store in Boiberik, sold out the stock and soon opened a dry-goods shop; we bargained for a piece of forest-land, took a few rubles for the option and backed off; we tried to buy the Anatovka meat tax concession*, made some money and decided to become money-lenders.

"My enemies should be so mad!" at last cried my wife. "You want to squander the few *groszy*** and have nothing left but a whip-handle?"

"What then? Do you think it's better to deal in grain and go bankrupt? Isn't it enough that the world is being beggared through wheat? Go and hear what's doing in Odessa!"

"What do I care about Odessa?" replied Golda. "My forefathers never set foot there and neither will my children as long as I am alive and my feet carry me."

"Then what do you want?" I asked her.

"What I want? I want you to stop playing the fool and talking nonsense."

"Of course," said I, "you're the wise one now; as they say, rubles give rise to thoughts, so if you are *maybe* going to get rich you are surely *already* wise. It's always so!"

Well, we quarreled and made it up several times, and at last we decided to buy, in addition to the cow we are getting for nothing, a real milch cow.

You probably want to ask me: why a cow and not a horse? So I'll answer: why a horse and not a cow? Boiberik is a place where all the wealthy Yehupetzers rent *dachas* for the summer, and since they are refined folk accustomed to having everything delivered ready-made to them, to be put straight into their mouths—firewood, meat, eggs, chickens, onions, pepper, parsley—then why shouldn't someone undertake to bring them cheese and butter and cream and so on? Seeing as the Yehupetzers are fond of food and their money is, you might say, a bastard, a good profit could be made from such a business. The main thing is to deliver good merchandise, and such wares as mine you wouldn't find even in Yehupetz. Both of us together should receive as many blessings as

---

*A special tax on *kosher* meat levied by the tsarist government. The right to collect it was granted to a concessionaire, a wealthy person who extorted the money from the Jewish population, making life especially hard for the poor.—*Tr.*
**A polish monetary unit equal to 1/100 zloty.—*Tr.*

the number of times important people, Gentiles, have implored me to bring them fresh dairy products: "We've heard, Tevye," they would say, "that you are an honest man, even though you are a scabby Jew." Do you think you'll get such a compliment from Jews? My enemies should waste away for as long as I'd have to wait for it! From our pettifoggers you don't get a good word. The only thing they know is to peer into someone else's pot. Seeing that Tevye has an extra cow and a new wagon they begin to rack their brains: from where and from what? Maybe this Tevye deals in counterfeit money? Or runs a still on the quiet?

Ha-ha-ha! Go on, brotherkins, rack your brains in good health! is what I think to myself.

I don't know whether you'll believe me, but you are almost the first person I've told the whole story to, just as it happened...

However, it seems to me that I've already talked a little too much. Please don't hold it against me, but we've both got to go about our own affairs, or, as the Bible says, *"Every crow to its own kind"*—to each his own. You to your books, I to my pots and jugs. But one request I will make: don't write me into one of your books, and if you do, then at least don't mention my real name... I wish you health and may everything always go well with you.

1894

27

Tevye, Golda, their seven daughters, and the cow.

The Soap Bubble

"There are many thoughts in a man's heart"—that's what it says, doesn't it, in our sacred Torah? I don't have to explain it to you, Reb Sholom Aleichem. In plain Yiddish we have a saying: "The best horse needs a whip, the wisest man—advice." Who do I mean? Myself, that's who, for had I had the sense to consult a good friend and tell him everything, I would surely not have gotten myself into such a pretty mess. *"Life and death issue from thine own lips"*—when God wishes to punish a man, He takes away his reason. How many times have I told myself: Just think, Tevye, you blockhead, people say that you aren't altogether a fool, how come you let yourself be taken in, and so stupidly? What would you have lost from the earnings—knock on wood—you make with your little dairy business that has won such a good reputation everywhere, in Boiberik, in Yehupetz, and far and wide? How fine and how sweet it would have been right now if your *mezumen* was lying quietly in a chest, safely hidden, without a human soul being aware of it! For who cares, I ask you, whether Tevye has any money or not? Indeed! Was the world much interested in Tevye when he lay sunken—such a fate shouldn't befall others—nine cubits deep in the ground, dying of hunger three times a day with his wife and children? Only later, when God took notice of Tevye and changed his luck all of a sudden, when Tevye somehow or other managed to build up a little business, when he began to save up a few rubles, only then did the world take heed, and plain Tevye became Reb Tevye—no kidding! Plenty of good friends appeared; as it is written in the Book: *"He is beloved by everyone"*—when God gives a spoonful, people offer bucketfuls. Each and everyone came along with his advice: this one said a dry-goods shop, that one—a grocery, this one—a house, an estate, landed property, another one said wheat, this one—timber, that one—auctioneering...

Brotherkins!" I told them. "Leave me alone! You are widely mistaken: you apparently think I am Brodsky. We should all have as much as I need to make up three hundred rubles, even two hundred, or even a hundred and fifty! Another's property is easy to count; it seems to glitter like gold, but when one comes up close it's only a brass button."

In short, may Heaven preserve them, our petty folk did finally put a "good" eye on me! God sent me a relative—such close kin that I couldn't have told him from a hole in the wall! Menachem-Mendel was his name, a rolling stone, a flighty gadabout, a twister, a good-for-nothing, may he never rest! He hooked on to me and turned my head with his fantasies, his castles-in-the-air. So you may well ask me: *"Wherefore did it come to pass?"* how did I, Tevye, fall in with Menachem-Mendel? The only justification I have is the passage from the *Haggadah* that says:... *"Slaves we were....,"* meaning so it was ordained. Here's the story.

I went to Yehupetz once at the beginning of winter with my bit of merchandise—over twenty pounds of fresh butter from butterland, a couple of bags of beautiful cottage cheese—gold and silver, we should both wish ourselves no worse! As you understand, I sold off my goods immediately, didn't leave myself a lick; I didn't even get to visit all of my summer customers, the Boiberik summer people who look forward to my coming as if I were the Messiah. And no wonder—they get sick and tired of your Yehupetz dealers who can by no means supply them with such goods as Tevye's. I don't have to tell you—as the prophet says: *"Let another praise thee."* Good merchandise is its own praise.

Well, I sold out all my wares, threw my horse a little hay and went for a stroll in the city. *"Man is born of dust and to dust he returneth"*—a man is no more than mortal, so he wants to take a look at the world, catch a breath of air, look at the rarities Yehupetz displays in its windows, as if saying: "With your eyes—as much as you like, but with your hands—don't you dare!"

Standing in front of a large window behind which there lay piles of gold half-imperials*, silver rubles and no end of all kinds of paper money I thought: God Almighty! If I had but a tenth part of what I see here what would I have to ask from God and who would be equal to me? First of all I'd find a match for my eldest daughter, give her a dowry of five hundred rubles in addition to bride-gifts, clothing and wedding expenses; my horse and wagon and the cows I would sell and move to the city, buy myself a seat by the Eastern

---

*A gold coin in the former Russian Empire. — *Tr.*

30

wall in the synagogue, and for my wife, God bless her, a few strings of pearls, and I would give out alms like the finest householder. I would see to it that the Temple got a new tin roof instead of standing, as it does now, roofless, ready to cave in any minute. I would set up a *Talmud-Torah* for the children and a hospital, as in all decent towns, so that poor people shouldn't have to huddle on the bare ground in the prayer-house, and I would immediately get rid of that brazen Yankel, the trustee of the burial society, and put an end to his guzzling vodka and chicken livers at the community's expense!

"*Sholom Aleichem,* Reb Tevye!" somebody called to me from behind my back. "How are you?"

I turned around and took a look—I could have sworn I knew his face! *"Aleichem Sholom,"* I answered, "where do you hail from?"

"From where? From Kasrilovka," he answered, "I'm a kinsman of yours, your wife Golda's own third cousin once removed."

"Hold on," said I, "aren't you a son-in-law of Boruch-Hirsch, Leah-Dvosya's husband?"

"Right you are," said he, "I am Boruch-Hirsch Leah-Dvosya's son-in-law, and my wife's name is Sheine-Sheindl, Boruch-Hirsch Leah-Dvosya's daughter, so now you already know me."

"Just a moment," said I, "your mother-in-law's grandmother, Sarah-Yenta, and my wife's aunt Frumeh-Zlata were, I seem to remember, first cousins, and if I am not mistaken, you are Boruch-Hirsch Leah-Dvosya's middle son-in-law, but I've forgotten what your name is, its slipped my mind somehow. What is your real name?"

"I am called," said he, "Menachem-Mendel Boruch-Hirsch Leah-Dvosya's, that's what they call me at home, in Kasrilovka."

"In that case, my dear Menachem-Mendel," said I to him, "I owe you an altogether different sort of greeting! Come, tell me, my precious Menachem-Mendel, what are you doing here, how are your mother-in-law and your father-in-law, long life to them? How is your health, how is your business getting along?"

"Eh," said he, "my health is, thank God, not bad, I live; but my business affairs aren't so good at present,"

"God will help you," said I, glancing at his threadbare clothes and worn-out shoes. "No matter, God will help you, things will probably get better. As the Book says, *All is vanity'*, money, I say, is round, today it rolls this way, tomorrow that way, the main thing is to go on living. What is most important is hope, a Jew must go

*"This one said a dry-goods shop, that one—a grocery, that one—a
house, an estate…another said wheat, this one—timber…."*

on hoping. What if you do suffer? After all, that's what we Jews are in this world for. As they say, if you're a soldier you must smell gunpowder. *'Man is likened to a broken pot'*—the whole world," said I, "is a dream. Better tell me, Menachem-Mendel, my good man, how you come to be here, all of a sudden, in Yehupetz?"

"What do you mean," he asked, "how I come to be here? I've been here already, little by little, for something like a year and a half."

"So you," said I, "are a local, a real Yehupetz resident?"

"Sh-sh-sh!!!" he exclaimed, glancing around in all directions, "don't shout so loudly, Reb Tevye; I do live here, but that's between you and me."

I stood there looking at him as if he were crazy, "You're a fugitive," said I, "and hiding yourself in the middle of the market-place?"

"Don't ask," said he, "Reb Tevye, that's the way it is. You, apparently, have no idea of the Yehupetz laws and customs... Come, I'll explain, so you'll understand how one can both *be* and *not be* a local resident." And he gave me a whole song and dance on the subject of how a person struggles for his life in Yehupetz.

"Listen to me, Menachem-Mendel, come with me to the village for one day," said I, "your bones, at least, will get a little rest. You'll be our guest, and a most welcome one, my old woman will be overjoyed."

In short, I talked him into coming with me. When we arrived—what jubilation! A guest! An own third cousin! No small matter, for blood, as they say, is thicker than water. My wife began to shower our guest with questions: what was new in Kasrilovka? How was Uncle Boruch-Hirsch? What was Aunt Leah-Dvosya doing? Uncle Yosl-Menashe? Aunt Dobrish? And how were their children getting along? Who had died? Who had gotten married? Who was divorced? Who had given birth and who was expecting?

"Of what use, my dear wife," said I, "are someone else's weddings or circumcisions to you? You'd better see to it that we have something to put into our mouths. *'All who are hungry enter and be fed'*—before eating one doesn't feel like dancing. If it's a borsht—well and good, if not—no matter, let it be *knishes* or *kreplakh*, stuffed or empty dumplings, or maybe even *blintzes* with cheese, or *vertutti*—anything you have, but make it quick."

Well, so we washed our hands and had a good meal, as you say: *"They ate"* and Rashi explains: "As God bade them."

33

"Eat, Menachem-Mendel," I urged him, "anyhow, as King David said, it is a *vanity of vanities.*' It's a foolish world and a false one, while, as my grandmother Nehameh of blessed memory used to say—she was a clever old woman, wondrously wise—it's in the bowl that health and pleasure are to be sought."

My poor guest—his hands even trembled—couldn't find enough words to praise my wife's cookery. He swore by all that was sacred that he couldn't remember when he had eaten such a wonderful dairy meal, such delicious *knishes* and *vertutti*.

"Don't be silly," said I, "if you'd had a taste of her bakery, or noodle pudding—you would then learn the meaning of Paradise on earth!"

Well, after we'd eaten and said our benedictions, the talk turned to what was uppermost in our minds; he spoke of his affairs, I—of this and that and another; he talked about his deals, told us stories about Odessa and Yehupetz, said that about ten times already he had been *na konye i pid konyom*—riding a horse and thrown from the horse—rich today, poor tomorrow, rich again and again a poor man. He dealt in some kind of stuff I had never in my life heard of, absurd and crazy sounding: *hos* and *bes*, shares-shmares, Potivilov, Maltzev-shmaltzev, the devil knows what they are, and the crazy figures he named, ten thousand, twenty thousand— money like firewood!

"I'll tell you the truth, Menachem-Mendel," said I, "from what you tell me of the ins and outs of your business I see it calls for real skill and know-how. But there's one thing I can't understand: since I am acquainted with your good lady it puzzles me greatly that she permits you to fly around so and doesn't come after you riding a broomstick!"

"Eh," said he with a sigh, "don't remind me of that, Reb Tevye, I get enough from her as it is, both cold and hot. You should only hear what she writes me, then you would say that I am a saintly man. But this," he went on, "is a small matter, you expect a wife to nag you to death. There is a much worse thing: I have, you must understand, a dear mother-in-law! I don't have to tell you—you know her yourself!"

"So with you," I say, "it's as the Bible says: *'The flocks were ringstraked, speckled and grisled',* which means a boil on a boil and a blister on the boil?"

"Yes, Reb Tevye," said he, "you've got it right; the boil is a boil, but the blister, oh, the blister is worse than the boil!"

Well, so we went on chatting until late at night. I was already quite dizzy from his yarns, from his crazy stories of the thousands of rubles that fly up and down, of Brodsky's wealth...All night long I dreamed of Yehupetz.... half-imperials...Brodsky... Menachem Mendel and his mother-in-law. Only in the morning did he get down to brass tacks; what, then? "Since," he said, "with us in Yehupetz cash has for some time now become preferable, while nobody cares a hoot for merchandise, therefore," said he, "you have a chance, Reb Tevye, to snatch yourself a goodly sum and at the same time literally save me, bring me back to life from the dead."

"Childish talk," said I to him, "you must think that I have the Yehupetz kind of money, half-imperials? You little fool," said I, "what I lack to be as rich as Brodsky we might both of us wish we could earn before Passover."

"Yes," said he, "that I know. But do you think a large sum is necessary for this? If you gave me a hundred today," he said, "I would turn it into two hundred in three-four days, into three hundred, six hundred, seven hundred and why not even a whole thousand?"

"It is quite possible," said I, "that it's as our Book says: *'The profit is great but it's far from my pocket!'* But what's the use of such talk? It's all very fine when there's something to invest—but when there is no hundred rubles it follows that *'alone you come in and alone you go out'* or as Rashi explains, when you plant a sickness you reap a fever."

"Eh, come on," said he, "I'm sure you can find a hundred rubles, Reb Tevye. With your business, your name, knock on wood!"

"What's in a name?" said I. "A name, naturally, is a good thing. But what of that? I remain with my name, while the money is all Brodsky's. If you want to know precisely, I'll tell you that I have all in all barely a hundred rubles, but I have eighteen holes to patch with this sum: first, to marry off a daughter..."

"Just listen to him," said he, "that's just the last to fit your shoe! Because when, Reb Tevye, will you have another such opportunity to invest one hundred and take out, God willing, enough for marrying off children, and for something else, too?"

And he went into a new three-hour-long harangue to let me understand how he makes three rubles out of one, and from three—ten. First of all, he said, you invest a hundred rubles and then you order ten somethings—I've already forgotten what they're called—to be bought for you; then you wait a few days until its price goes up. Then you send off a telegram somewhere with an order to sell, and with the money, to buy twice as much; then the price goes up again and you dispatch another telegram; this goes on until the hundred becomes two hundred, the two hundred—four hundred, the four—eight, the eight—sixteen hundred, real *"miracles and wonders"!* There are people, he said, in Yehupetz, who just recently walked around barefoot, they were brokers, messengers, servants, today they live in their own brick houses, their wives complain of stomach ailments and go abroad for treatment. They themselves dash around in Yehupetz on rubber wheels—hoity-toity, they don't recognize people any more!

Well, why drag out the story? He got me hooked. Who knows, I thought, maybe he was sent to me by fate? After all, I do hear that people find their luck in Yehupetz with the aid of their five fingers—am I any worse than they? He doesn't seem to be a liar who thinks up such songs out of his head. What if my luck really does, thought I, take a turn in the right direction and Tevye becomes something of a person in his old age at least? Really, when will the end come to my struggles, my exhaustive drudgery? Day in and day out again the horse and wagon, and again cheese and butter. It's time, Tevye, to take a rest, I told myself, to become a somebody, to go to the prayer house, to look into a sacred book. But what if, God forbid, things should go wrong, that is, fall buttered side down? Better not to think of that!

"Well? What do you think?" I asked my old woman. "How do you like his plan, Golda?"

"What can I say?" she replied, "I know that Menachem-Mendel is not, God forbid, just anybody, he won't hoodwink you. He does not come from any tailors or cobblers! His father is a very upright person, and he had a grandfather who was really a jewel: he sat day and night studying the Torah, even after he went blind. And Grandmother Tzeitl, may she rest in peace, was also no simple woman,"

"It's a fable about *Hanukkah* lights in the summer," said I, "we're talking business, and here she comes along with her grandmother Tzeitl who baked honey-cakes, and with her grandfather who lost his soul in a wine-glass... A woman is always a woman. It's not for nothing that King Solomon traveled the world over and couldn't find a woman with a rivet in her head."

In short, we agreed to set up a partnership: I invest the money

36

and Menachem-Mendel his wits, and whatever God sent us we would divide half and half.

"Believe me, Reb Tevye," he said, "I'll make a fine deal for you, God willing, as fine as fine can be, and with God's help will bring you money and money and more money!"

"Amen, the same to you," said I, "from your mouth into God's ears. But there is one thing I don't understand: how does the cat get over the water? I am here, you are there; money is a delicate material, see? Don't take offense, but as our Forefather Abraham said: *'If you sow with tears you shall reap with joy'*—it is better to make sure beforehand than to weep afterwards."

"Oh," said he to me, "maybe you want us to sign a paper? With the greatest pleasure!"

"Shush," said I, "if you look at it another way, it comes to the same thing: it's either or; if you want to kill me, of what use will a piece of paper be to me? As it is written in the Talmud: *'The thief is not the mouse, but the mousehole'*— it isn't the note that pays but the man, and if I already hang by one foot let me hang by both."

"You may believe me," he said, "Reb Tevye, I swear to you on my most holy word of honor, so help me God, I haven't the slightest intention of duping you, God forbid; everything will be aboveboard and honest. God willing, we'll divide everything equally, half and half, share and share alike, a hundred for me, a hundred for you, two hundred for me, two hundred for you, three hundred for me, three hundred for you, four hundred for me, four hundred for you, a thousand for me, a thousand for you."

Well, so I got out my few rubles, counted them over three times—my hands trembled as I counted—called my old woman to be a witness, made it clear once more what blood money this was and gave it to Menachem-Mendel; I sewed it up into his breast pocket so it shouldn't, God forbid, be stolen on the way, and we decided that no later than next Saturday week he would, without fail, write me a full account of our affairs. We took hearty leave of each other, embraced and kissed each other as is usual among relatives.

When I was alone all sorts of sweet thoughts passed through my mind, all kinds of daydreams, so pleasant that I wished they would never end. I saw a large, tin-roofed house in the middle of town, a real mansion with sheds and stables and stalls, with large and small chambers, with pantries full of good things, and I saw the mistress of the house jingling her keys as she flitted from room to room—and she was my wife Golda, but unrecognizable: her face has changed, it has become the face of a wealthy woman, with a double chin and pearls strung around her neck; she gives herself airs and curses the maids vehemently; my children go around in their best clothes doing nothing. The yard is flocked with chickens, geese and ducks. Inside the house everything is bright, a fire flickers in the oven, supper is cooking and the samovar is puffing as it boils merrily! At the head of the table sits the master of the house, Tevye, that is. He is wearing a houserobe and a skullcap, around him sit the most prominent men of the town fawning on him, cringing before him: "If you please, Reb Tevye, no offense meant, Reb Tevye..."

"Oh," thought I, "money—the devil take your fathers and forefathers!"

"Whom are you cursing so?" asked my Golda.

"Nobody, I was merely thinking, daydreaming, seeing visions—ah, hopeless things... Tell me, Golda my love," said I, "do you know what he deals in, this relative of yours, Menachem-Mendel?"

"What I dreamed the other night and last night and this whole year should fall on the heads of my enemies! You sat up with the man a day and a night talking and talking and talking, and then you come to me and ask me what he deals in! You made up some sort of an agreement with him, didn't you?"

"Yes," said I, "we did make up something, but what it is I don't know, not for the life of me! There's nothing, you see, to get hold of; however, one thing has nothing to do with the other, don't you worry, my dear wife, my heart tells me that everything will turn out well and we, with God's help, so it seems to me, will earn money, and lots of it—so say 'Amen' and cook supper!"

Well, a week went by, and then another, and still another—no letters from my partner! I was beside myself, I lost my head and didn't know what to think. It can't be, thought I, that he should simply forget to write a letter; he knows quite well how anxiously we await it here. But then again another thought struck me: what will I do to him if he, for instance, skims the entire cream for himself and tells me that we haven't earned anything yet! Go tell him he's a so-and-so!? But it can't be, I told myself, how is it possible? I treat a man as I would a close and dear relative, I should only have what I wish for him, so how can he play such a trick on me? Then another thought struck me: the devil take the profit, let it be

38

his, *"Deliverance and protection will come from the Lord"*—may God save my investment from harm! A chill ran through my body.

You old fool, I said to myself, you already prepared a purse, you dunce! For the hundred rubles you could have brought yourself a pair of horses the likes of which your ancestors never owned and exchanged your wagon for a spring-hung britzka!

"Tevye, why don't you think of something!" cried my wife.

"What do you mean—I don't think? My head is bursting from thinking," said I, "and you say I don't think!"

"Something must have happened to him on the way," said she. "Either he was waylaid by robbers and cleaned out from head to toe, or he fell sick on the way, or, God forbid, maybe even died."

"What else, dear heart, will you think up?" I asked her. "Suddenly robbers out of the blue!" But I myself thought: Who knows what could happen to a man on the road?

"You, my wife, always have to think the very worst!"

"Well," said she, "he comes from that kind of a family. His mother, may she be our defender in Heaven, died not long ago, still a young woman; he had three sisters, so one of them died in her girlhood, the other one did get married, but caught a cold in the bath-house and died, while the third one lost her mind right after her first confinement, lingered on for some time and then died."

"All life ends in death," said I, "we'll all be dead some day, Golda. A man is like a carpenter: a carpenter lives and lives and dies, and a man lives and dies."

In short, we decided that I should go to Yehupetz. A bit of my stock-in-trade had accumulated by this time, a shopful of cheese and butter and cream, all of prime quality. We harnessed the horse and, as Rashi says: *"They journeyed from Sukos."* On to Yehupetz!

As I drove along, despondent, of course, heavy-hearted, as you may well imagine, all alone in the woods, all sorts of notions and thoughts entered my mind.

Now won't it be a fine thing, I thought, if when I arrive and start asking about my man I hear: "Menachem-Mendel? Oho-ho! That one is in clover, has his own brick house, drives around in carriages, is not to be recognized at all!" So I pluck up courage and go directly to his house. "Whoa!" somebody exclaims at the entrance and gives me a hard shove with an elbow. "Don't push so, man, this is no place for pushing." "I am," I say, "a kinsman, my wife is his third cousin once removed." *"Mazl-tov,"* he answers, "a great pleasure; however, it won't hurt you to wait here by the door a while..." It dawns on me that the doorman should be tipped... As they say, *"What goes up must come down"*—meaning that the wheels won't turn if the axle isn't greased. And that the wheels won't turn if the axle isn't greased. And then I go straight upstairs to Menachem-Mendel and say: "A good morning to you, Reb Menachem-Mendel!" Who? What? *"There is no speech, there are no words."* "He doesn't recognize me at all! "What do you want?" he asks. I almost faint.

"What does this mean, Mister, you no longer recognize relatives? I am Tevye."

"Oh," says he, "Tevye? The name seems familiar..."

"Then maybe," say I, "my wife's *blintzes* are also familiar to you, remind yourself of her *knishes,* dumplings and *vertutti!*"

Then quite different thoughts come to my mind: here I come in to Menachem-Mendel and he gives me a most hearty welcome, "A guest! A guest! Sit down, Reb Tevye, how are you, how is your wife? I've been looking forward to your arrival, I want to settle our accounts." And then he takes and pours me a hatful of gold coins. "This," he says, "is the profit, and the principal stays in the business; whatever we earn we'll divide in half, share and share alike, a hundred for me, a hundred for you, two hundred for me, two hundred for you, three hundred for me, three hundred for you, four hundred for me, four hundred for you." So thinking I get a bit drowsy and don't notice that my nag has strayed from the road; the cart catches on a tree, and I get such a jolt from behind that sparks fly from my eyes. It's a good thing, say I to myself, that at least no axle broke, thank God.

Well, at last I got to Yehupetz. First of all I sold off my goods very quickly, as I usually do, and then I went about looking for my partner.

I wander around for an hour, two, and three, but *"the lad is gone"*—I can't find him! I begin stopping people, asking them whether they'd heard of or seen a man with the lovely name of Menachem-Mendel? "If," they say, "his name is Menachem-Mendel you should look for him with a candle; this isn't enough," they say, "there are lots of Menachem-Mendels in the world." "You probably mean his family name?" say I, "Let me know as much evil, with you together, if, all told, he isn't called—at home, in Kasrilovka—by his mother-in-law's name alone, that is,

Menachem-Mendel Leah-Dvosya's. What's more, his father-in-law, already a very old man, is also called by her name—Boruch-Hirsch Leah-Dvosya's, and even she herself, Leah-Dvosya, that is, is known as Leah-Dvosya Boruch-Hirsch Leah-Dvosya's. Do you understand now?"

"We understand," they say, "but all this is still not enough; what is his business, what does he do, your Menachem-Mendel?"

"What is his business? He does business here with half-imperial gold pieces, some sore of *'bess-mess'*, Potivilov, sends telegrams someplace—to Petersburg, to Warsaw," I explain.

"Oh!" they cry and rock with laughter. "Do you mean the Menachem-Mendel who sells last year's snow? Go, if you please, down over there—to the other side of the street; that's where lots of hares run around, and yours among them."

The more one lives, the more one eats, think I to myself, so now it's hares!? Last year's snow!?

So I crossed to the other side. There were so many people there, may no evil befall them, as at a fair; the crowd was so dense that I barely pushed myself through. People ran around like madmen, one this way, the other that way, bumping into each other, a real Bedlam with everyone talking, screaming, waving their hands: "Potivilov..." "Done, done!" "Caught you at your word!" "Shoved in a down payment... it'll scratch..." "You owe me brokerage..." "You're a rat... you'll get your head smashed..." "Spit in his face..." "Just look—a real kill!" "A fine speculator..." "Bankrupt!" "Flunkey!" "A curse on you and your ancestors!" Now slaps were about to fly in earnest.

"Jacob fled," I muttered to myself, "run away, Tevye, or you'll catch a few slaps yourself!"

Well, well, I reflected, God is a Father, Shmuel-Shmelki is his servitor, Yehupetz is a city and Menachem-Mendel is a breadwinner! So this is the spot where people catch fortunes, half-imperials? This Bedlam is what they call doing business? Alas and alack, Tevye, with your commercial deals!

To make a long story short, when I stopped in front of a great big show-window displaying all kinds of trousers I suddenly saw, reflected in the glass, my lost partner. When I looked at him my heart missed a beat, I felt faint. If I have an enemy anywhere, or if you have one, let us both live to see them looking the way

41

"When I looked at him, my heart missed a beat, I felt faint."

Menachem-Mendel looked! A coat? Boots? And his face—why, my God, healthier-looking corpses are laid to rest.

Well, Tevye, now you are really done for, I thought to myself, you can say goodbye to your little nest egg, as they say: There is neither bear nor forest—neither stock nor money, nothing but troubles...

He, evidently, was also greatly embarrassed, because we both stopped as if frozen and couldn't utter a word; we only looked right into each other's eyes, as roosters do, as if to say: "Both of us are hapless unfortunates, we might as well take up our sacks and go begging from house to house!"

"Reb Tevye," he said in a low voice, barely managing to speak, choking with tears, "Reb Tevye! Without luck one shouldn't be born at all... rather than such a life... be hanged... drawn and quartered!" And not another word could he utter.

"Of course," I said to him, "for this deed of yours, Menachem-Mendel, you deserve to be laid out right here in the middle of Yehupetz and flogged until you see grandmother Tzeitl in the other world. Just think what you've gone and done! You've taken an entire household of living people, innocent, unhappy people, and cut their throats without a knife! Oh God, how will I come home now to my wife and children? Come on, tell me yourself, you murderer, robber, cutthroat!"

"It's true," said he, leaning against a wall, "it's true, Reb Tevye, so help me God..."

"Gehenna, you fool," said I, "Gehenna is too good for you!"

"All true, Reb Tevye," said he, "all true, so help me God; rather than such a life, such a life, Reb Tevye..." and he hung his head.

I stood there looking at him, the *shlimazl*, as he was leaning against the wall, his head bent, his hat awry, and every sigh and every groan tore at my heart.

"Although," said I "if we look at it another way, then it becomes quite clear that maybe you are also innocent; let us examine the matter from all sides: did you do this with malice aforethought? But it would be foolish to think so, you were my partner on equal share-and-share alike terms; I put in the money, you put in your brains, woe is me! Your intention was for the best, for life and not for death, as the saying goes. Oh, so it turned out to be a soap bubble? It was probably not ordained; as it is said; *'Don't rejoice today because tomorrow...'* Man proposes and God disposes. Look, you little fool, take my bit of business—it's a solvent business; still, as I say, since it was then so ordained, Heaven preserve us, last autumn one of my cows—it shouldn't happen to you—lay down and died; it could have brought in a bargain—fifty rubles if sold for *treif* meat; directly after that a red heifer fell, I wouldn't have considered taking even twenty rubles for it—well, so what can you do, wits won't help. If you're out of luck you're lost!

"I won't even ask you where my money is," I said. "I understand very well where it went, my blood money, woe is me! It's in a sacred place, in last year's snow. And whose fault is it if not mine? I let myself be talked into reaching out for easy money, stuff and nonsense... Money, brother, must be toiled for, slaved for, worked to the bone for! You deserve a good thrashing, Tevye, you do! But of what use is my crying now? As the Book says: *'The maiden screamed'*—scream yourself blue! Wit and remorse—these two things always come too late. It wasn't fated that Tevye should become a rich man. As Ivan says: *Nye bulo u Mikiti hroshi i nye budye*—no money had Mikita and none will he have. Evidently that's God's will. *'The Lord giveth and the Lord taketh away,'* Rashi explains. Come, brother," said I, "we'll take a few drops of vodka!"

And so, Mr. Sholom Aleichem, all my dreams turned out to be a soap bubble! Do you think I took it to heart and grieved over the loss of my money? May I be as free from evil! We know what the Good Book says: *"The silver and the gold are mine"*—money is mud! The main thing is man, that is, that a person should be a real human being. But what did grieve me? My lost dream. I wanted, oh, how I wanted to be a rich man at least for a while. But is wisdom of any use in this? *"Perforce you must live,"* says the proverb—with groans you live and with groans you wear out a pair of boots. You, Tevye, says God, should keep your mind on cheese and butter and not on daydreams. But faith, hope? The more troubles, the more faith, the poorer one is the greater are his hopes. From this it follows...

But it seems to me that I've talked too much today. It's time to think of my business. As they say, each one has his own scourges.

Fare you well, be healthy and happy always!

1895

Today's Children

You said "today's children"? *I have raised children*—you bring them into the world, sacrifice yourself for them, toil day and night, and for what? You think maybe it'll come out right this way or maybe that way, according to your own notions and means. I can't compare with Brodsky, of course, but neither am I just anybody, believe me: we don't come, as my wife, bless her, says, from tailors or cobblers, so I reckoned that I'd draw winning numbers with my daughters. Why? Firstly, God blessed me with good-looking girls, and a pretty face, as you say, is half a dowry. Secondly, I am now, with God's help, no longer the Tevye of former times, so I can aim for the finest match even in Yehupetz—what will you say to that? Yes, but there is a God in the world, a Merciful Father who shows his great miracles and makes me hot and cold, tosses me up and down. So he says to me: "Tevye, don't talk yourself into any foolishness and let the world go on as it does!.." Just listen to what can happen in our big world, and who gets all the luck. Tevye the *shlimazl!*

To make a long story short—you probably remember what happened to me, may this never happen to you, the story with my kinsman Menachem-Mendel, may his name and remembrance be erased, our fine deal in Yehupetz with the half-imperials and the "Potivilov" shares, such a year on my enemies! How I grieved then! I thought this was the end, no more Tevye, no more dairy business!

"What a fool you are," my old woman said one day, "stop your worrying, nothing good will come of it! You'll only eat your heart out. Look at it as if you'd been waylaid by highwaymen and robbed clean. Better take a walk to Anatovka, go see Leizer-Wolf the butcher, he is very anxious, he says, to see you."

"What does he need me for? If he is thinking of that dun-colored cow of ours," said I, "he may as well take a big stick and beat the idea out of his head."

45

"Why so?" she asked. "Is it the milk you get from her, or the cheese and butter?"

"It's not that," said I, "it's the idea in general. It would be a sin to give such a cow away to be slaughtered; 'A pity for living things,' says our Holy Torah."

"Oh, stop it, Tevye! The whole world knows that you are a bookish man. Listen to me, your wife," said she, "and go and visit Leizer-Wolf. Every Thursday when our Tzeitl goes to his butcher shop for meat he pesters her: 'Tell your father he should come and see me. I have some important business to discuss with him.'"

In short, once in a while a man must mind his wife, mustn't he? So, thinking it over, I let myself be talked into going to Leizer-Wolf in Anatovka, a walk of about three versts. I came to his place, but he wasn't at home. "Where is he?" I asked a snub-nosed woman who was flitting about the house.

"He's in the slaughterhouse," she answered, "they're slaughtering an ox there since early morning. He should soon be home."

I wandered around Leizer-Wolf's home admiring its fittings. A household, knock on wood, after my own heart; a cupboard full of copperware, couldn't be bought with a hundred and fifty rubles, a samovar, another samovar, a brass tray, another tray from Warsaw, a pair of silver candlesticks, large and small gilded goblets and cups, a cast-iron *Hanukkah* lamp, and many other things, all kinds of trinkets without end.

God Almighty! I thought, I should only live to see my children, bless them, have so many fine things! What a lucky man the butcher is! It's not enough that he is so rich, so he has to have only two children of his own, already married off, and be a widower into the bargain!

At last the door opened and in stomped Leizer-Wolf, hurling curses at the *shokhet's* head. The slaughterer had ruined him, he had rejected an ox as big as an oak-tree, declared it *treif* over a mere trifle, found a pinhead blemish on a lung, may the Evil One catch him!

"Good day, Reb Tevye," he said, "why is it so hard to get you to come here? How do you do?"

"I do and I do and get nowhere. As the Book says: *'I want not your honey and want not your sting'*—neither money, nor health, nor life and soul."

"It's a sin to talk so, Reb Tevye," said he, "as compared to what you once were you are today, knock on wood, a rich man."

"We should both have what I still need to be as rich as you think I am. But no matter, *'Ascacurdeh demaskanteh desnubnoseh defercloseh**, as it is written in the *Gemara,*" said I, thinking: more fool you, butcher-boy, if there's such a *Gemara* in the world!

"You're always ready with the *Gemara,*" said Leizer-Wolf. "You are lucky, Reb Tevye, to be skilled in reading the tiny letters. But how do knowledge and learning concern us? Let us better talk of our business. Sit down, Reb Tevye." As he said this he shouted: "Let there be tea!" And as if by magic the snub-nosed woman suddenly sprang from somewhere, snatched up the samovar as the devil snatched the *melamed,* and vanished into the kitchen.

"Now," said he to me, "when we are alone, eye to eye, we can talk business. For some time already I've wanted to have a talk with you, Reb Tevye, and I've asked you many times, through your daughter, to take the trouble... See, I've cast an eye..."

"I know," said I, "that you've cast an eye, but your efforts are all in vain, it won't go, Reb Leizer-Wolf."

"Why so?" he asked and looked at me as if scared.

"Because," said I, "I can afford to wait a while, the river hasn't caught on fire yet."

"Why should you wait when we can come to an agreement at once?" he asked.

"That," said I, "is firstly. And secondly, I'm sorry for the poor creature. *A pity for living things!*"

"Just look at him, how he takes on!" laughed Leizer-Wolf. "If somebody heard you he would swear that she was your only one! It seems to me, Reb Tevye, that you have knock on wood, plenty of them!"

"So let them be," said I, "and let whoever envies me have none."

"Envies you?" he asked in surprise. "Who speaks of envy? Quite the opposite, just because they are so fine I want... You understand? Don't forget, Reb Tevye, what favors you may get out of it!"

"Oh, of course, of course," said I, "your favors can turn a head to stone. You won't grudge a piece of ice in the winter, that we've known for a long time."

"Eh," said he in a honey-sweet voice, "why do you compare, Reb Tevye, then with now? Things were somewhat different *then,*

---

*Words without meaning —abracadabra. —*Tr.*

47

and *now* they're different again. Now we're becoming sort of kin, aren't we?"

"What kinship are you talking about?" I asked.

"Ordinary—in-laws!"

"What do you mean, Reb Leizer-Wolf, what are we talking about?"

"No, you tell me, Reb Tevye, what we are talking about."

"What do you mean," said I, "we're talking about my dun-colored cow that you want to buy!"

"Ha-ha-ha!!" Leizer-Wolf rolled with laughter. "A fine piece of cow, and dun-colored to boot, ha-ha-ha!!!"

"But then what did you mean, Reb Leizer-Wolf? Go ahead, tell me, so I'll laugh too."

"It's about your daughter, your Tzeitl, we've been talking all the time! You know, of course, Reb Tevye, it shouldn't happen to you, that I'm a widower. I thought the matter over and decided that there was no need for me to look for luck among strangers, have dealings with matchmakers, with the devil knows whom, when here we are both on the spot. I know *you* and you know *me*, I like the girl herself, too—I see her every Thursday in my shop, I've spoken with her a few times, she's a nice, quiet girl. As for me, you see for yourself that I'm no poor man, I have my own house, a couple of stores, a few hides up in the attic and some money in the chest as well; what need is there, Reb Tevye, to make difficulties for each other, to play games with each other? Let's just shake hands on it, one-two-three, do you get me or not?"

In short, when he had had his say I sat there speechless, as one who suddenly receives upsetting news. My first thought was: Leizer-Wolf... Tzeitl... He has children her age... But soon I stopped myself: Just imagine, such luck! Such a lucky thing for her! She'll have anything she wants! Well, what if he is a bit tight-fisted? In our times this is supposed to be the greatest virtue: *"Man's closest friend is he himself."* When you're good for others you're bad for yourself. His only real drawback is that he is a bit common. Well, all right, not everyone can be a scholar. There are plenty of rich men, fine men, in Anatovka, in Mazepovka, and even in Yehupetz who can't tell a cross from an *alef*. Still, since it is so ordained, let me have as good a year as the respect they draw from the world. As the Book says: *"You can't build without a foundation,"* which means that learning lies in a strong-box while wisdom is in the purse.

"Well, Reb Tevye," said he, "why are you silent?"

"Should I yell?" I asked, pretending to hesitate. "This, Reb Leizer-Wolf, is a matter that calls for reflection. It's no joke, she's my first-born child."

"On the other hand," said he, "just because she's your first-born you will be able to marry off a second daughter, too, and later on a third, you get me?"

"Amen, the same to you!" said I. "There's no big deal in marrying off a child, let God only send each her predestined one."

"Oh, no, Reb Tevye," said he, "I mean something altogether different, for, thank God, you don't have to worry about a dowry for your Tzeitl—everything a girl needs for her wedding, clothing and so on, I take upon myself, and something will find its way into your purse, too..."

"Fie, shame on you!" I cried. "You're talking, begging your pardon, as if you were in your butcher shop! What do you mean—into my purse? Fie! My Tzeitl is not the sort of girl, God forbid, that I should have to sell for money, fie, fie!!"

"If you say 'fie'—let it be 'fie'," said he, "I meant for the best, but if you say 'fie' let it be 'fie.' If it suits you it suits me! The main thing is that it should be as soon as possible, I need a mistress in the house, you get me?"

"I won't raise any objections, but my spouse has to be talked with," said I, "in such matters she takes the lead. It's no trifle. As Rashi says, *'Rachel weeps for her sons'*—the mother covers everything. Then she herself, Tzeitl, should also be asked. As they say, all the in-laws were taken to the wedding but the bridegroom was left at home!"

"Nonsense," said he, "you shouldn't ask—you should *tell*, Reb Tevye. Go home and tell them what is what and set up the wedding canopy—a couple of words and drink a toast to wet the deal!"

"Don't speak that way, Reb Leizer-Wolf, a girl is no widow, God forbid."

"Naturally," said he, "a girl is a girl, not a widow, and for that reason everything must be settled beforehand—clothing, this, that and other matters. Meanwhile, Reb Tevye, let's take a few drops to warm ourselves, what do you say?"

"With pleasure," said I, "why not? As the saying goes, Adam is a man and vodka is vodka. We have a *Gemara* in which it is written..." And I rattled off a *"Gemara,"* a sheer invention, something

49

from the *Song of Songs* and from the *Song of the Kid.*

Well, so we imbibed the bitter drops, as God bade us. Meanwhile the snub-nosed woman brought in the samovar and we fixed ourselves a couple of glasses of punch. The time passed merrily, we congratulated each other, talked, babbled about the match, mentioned this and that and again the match.

"Do you know, Reb Leizer-Wolf, what a gem she is?"

"I know," he said, "believe me, I know. If I hadn't known I wouldn't have spoken at all!"

Both of us spoke at the same time. I shouted: "A gem, a diamond! You should only know how to take good care of her, not to show the butcher in you..."

And he: "Don't worry, Reb Tevye, what she will eat at my table on weekdays she never had in your house on holidays..."

"Come on," said I, "food is not all that important. The rich man doesn't eat gold coins, nor the poor man—stones. You are a coarse person, so you won't be able to appreciate her housewifery, her *hallah*-baking, her fish, Reb Leizer-Wolf, her fish! It's a real privilege..."

To this he said: "Reb Tevye, you are, excuse me, already played out, you don't know people, you don't know me..."

"You put gold on one scale and Tzeitl on the other and they'll balance!" I shouted. "Listen, Reb Leizer-Wolf, even if you had your two hundred thousand you wouldn't be worth the heel of her foot anyhow!"

"Believe me, Reb Tevye, you are a great fool, even though you are older than I am!.."

In short, we must have yelled at each other in this manner for quite a while and we drank ourselves tipsy, so when I came home it was already late in the night and my feet felt as if they were shackled.

My wife, bless her, immediately guessed that I was soused and gave me a good dressing down.

"Hush, Golda, don't scold," I said quite cheerfully, almost ready to dance a jig, "stop shouting, dearest one, we should be congratulated!"

"On what joyous event?" she asked. "For having sold the dun-colored cow, poor thing, to Leizer-Wolf?"

"Worse!"

"Exchanged it for another cow? Hoodwinked poor Leizer-Wolf?"

"Still worse!"

"Come on, say something, just see how a word has to be squeezed out of him!" she shouted angrily.

"*Mazl-tov* to you, Golda," I repeated, "we must both be congratulated, our Tzeitl is betrothed!"

"In that case you're really good and drunk and no joke! You must've had quite a glassful somewhere!"

"I had a few drops of vodka with Leizer-Wolf, and he and I also drank a few glasses of punch, but I'm still in my right mind," I said. "Know, brother Golda, that our Tzeitl has become engaged, in a lucky hour, to Leizer-Wolf himself!"

And I told her the whole story from beginning to end; how, and why, and when, everything we had talked about, without missing the slightest detail.

"Listen, Tevye," said my wife, "God should always help me wherever I go—my heart told me that it wasn't for nothing that Leizer-Wolf summoned you! But I was afraid to think about it, afraid it might, God forbid, all come to naught. I thank Thee, my dear God, my kind and faithful Father, only let it all be in a good hour, an auspicious hour, and may she grow old with him in honor and riches, because Frumeh-Soreh, may she rest in peace, didn't have too good a life with him. She was, may she forgive me, an embittered woman, couldn't get along with anyone, not at all like our Tzeitl, a long life to her. I thank Thee, thank Thee, dear God!.. Well, Tevye, what did I tell you, you noodlehead? Does a person have to worry? When it's destined, it comes straight home to you..."

"Quite true, there's a proverb that clearly says..."

"What do I need your proverbs for," she said, "we have to think about getting ready for the wedding now. First of all, make a list for Leizer-Wolf of everything Tzeitl will need for her wedding; she hasn't even a stitch of underthings, not even a pair of stockings, you tell him. Then—clothes. She needs a silken gown for the wedding, a woolen dress for summer, another for winter, a couple of cotton house-dresses, petticoats, and I want her to have two coats: a cat-pelt burnoose for weekdays and a good one, with ruffles, for the Sabbath; then—hook-up boots on high heels, shoes, a corset, gloves, handkerchiefs, an umbrella and all the other things a girl must have in these times."

"How come, Golda darling," I asked, "that you know about all this nonsense?"

"Why not?" she retorted, "didn't I live among people? Or perhaps I never saw, when I lived at home in Kasrilovka, how people dressed? You let me talk everything over with him; Leizer-Wolf is a wealthy man, he won't like to be bothered by the whole world. If you eat pork, let the fat at least run down your beard."

To make a long story short, we talked in this way until daybreak.

"Well, my wife," I said at last, "go and put together the bits of cheese and butter you have and I'll set out for Boiberik. All is well and good, but the business can't be put aside, as the Book says: *'Man's soul belongs to God,'* meaning that his body is on earth."

It was still dark when I hitched my horse and wagon and set off for Boiberik. When I arrived at the marketplace in Boiberik— oh, my! Can there be a secret among Jews? Everybody already knew everything and congratulations were showered on me from all sides.

"Mazl-tov, Reb Tevye! When, God willing, is the wedding?"

"The same to you," said I, "it's as the saying goes: the father hasn't been born yet but his son has already grown up on the roof."

"Nonsense, Tevye, you'll have to stand us a drink; knock on wood, such luck, you've struck it rich—a gold mine!"

"The gold can give out, what remains is a hole in the ground!"

However, not wanting to be a swine and begrudge my friends a treat, I said: "As soon as I get through with all my Yehupetz customers I'll stand you some drinks and eats, we'll have a fling, and that'll be that, which means *'merriment and enjoyment'*—even beggars may celebrate!"

I got through with my business very quickly, as I usually do, and then treated a bunch of good friends to a few drinks. We wished each other luck, as is proper among people, and I set off for home in a lively mood, half-seas over. The sun shone hotly on this fine summer day, but the shadows of the trees protected me from the heat on both sides, and the scent of the pines was as balm to the soul. I stretched out like a lord in my wagon and let the horse have the reins; plod along, old friend, I said, you know the way home yourself. As we trundled along I raised my voice in song; I was in such a festive mood that I sang the tunes sung on the High Holidays from *Rosh Hashono* to *Yom Kippur.* Lying on my back, I looked up into the sky, while my thoughts were here on earth. The Heavens, I thought, are for God, while the Earth he gave to the *Children of Adam,* they should bash their heads against walls, fight as the cats do for great "luxuries," fight for being appointed *gabeh,* for honors and seniority in reading the Torah and lessons from the *Prophets* in the synagogue... *"The dead cannot praise God..."* People don't understand how they should praise God for the favors He confers on them... But we, poor folk, when we have one good day we thank and praise the Lord and say *"A'ave"*— I love Him, for He hearkens to my voice and my pleas, He inclines His ear to me when poverty and afflictions surround me on all sides. Here a cow suddenly lies down and dies, then a devil brings along a relative, a *shlimazl,* a Menachem-Mendel from Yehupetz who takes my last ruble, and I already think that I am done for, this is the end of the world, there is no truth on earth. What does God do? He sends Leizer-Wolf the idea to take my Tzeitl as she stands, without a dowry, and therefore I will double my praises to You, dear God, for having looked at Tevye and come to his aid. Let me have proud pleasure from my child, when I come to visit her, God willing, and see her as the mistress of a wealthy home, all found for her, closets full of linen, well-stocked pantries with Passover chicken fat and preserves, coops full of chickens, geese and ducks...

Suddenly my horse made a dash downhill, and before I knew it I found myself lying on the ground amidst all the empty crocks and pots and the wagon on top of me! With difficulty and pain I managed to crawl out from under the wagon and get to my feet, bruised and half-dead. My wrath I vented on the poor horse. "Damn you," I shouted, "may the earth swallow you! Who asked you, *shlimazl,* to show that you can run downhill? You almost made a cripple of me, you *Asmodeus."* I gave it to him good and hard—as much as he could take. The poor animal evidently understood his mischief had gone too far: he stood with his head hanging low as if ready to be milked.

"The Evil One take you," said I and uprighted the wagon, picked up all the pots and crocks, and continued on my way.

It's a bad omen, I said to myself, hoping no new misfortune had happened at home...

Yes, *"So it was."* I drove along for about two versts and was already near home when I noticed somebody walking towards me in the middle of the road—a woman. I got a little closer—Tzeitl! I don't know why, but my heart felt as if it were sinking. I jumped off the wagon: "Tzeitl, is it you? What are you doing here?"

She fell on my neck, weeping loudly. "God be with you, daughter," said I, "why are crying?"

"Oh," she answered, "Father, *Tateh!*" Her face was bathed in tears.

The light went out of my eyes and my heart contracted painfully.

"What is it, daughter, what's happened to you? I asked and put my arms around her, stroking and kissing her. But she went on crying: "Father, dear Father, kind Father, I'll eat only one piece of bread in three days, have compassion for my youth!" And again she was choked with tears, couldn't utter another word.

Woe is me, I thought, I see where the land lies. It was an ill wind that took me to Boiberik!

"Silly little girl," I said, stroking her head, "why should you cry? It's either one or the other—no is no. Nobody, God forbid, is going to force you against your will. We thought it was for your good, we meant it for the best. But if your heart is not in it—what can be done? It probably wasn't ordained..."

"Oh, thank you, dear Father," she cried, "a long life to you." And once again she fell on my neck and started weeping, shedding tears.

"Listen, let there already be an end to this weeping," said I, "even eating meat dumplings can become tiresome! Get into the wagon and let's go home, your mother will be thinking God knows what!"

So we both got into the wagon and I began to calm her down with talk. I told her that we had the best of intentions; God knows the truth, all we wanted was to shield our child from misery. Well, it's come to nothing—evidently, such was God's will.

"It wasn't fated, daughter," I said, "that you should become the mistress of a wealthy home, and that we should reap a little joy in our old age, harnessed as we are, one might say, day and night to a wheelbarrow, not a good moment, only poverty and misery, bad luck over and over again!"

"Oh, *Tateh,*" she cried and again began to shed tears. "I'll go out and be a servant, I'll carry clay, I'll dig ditches!.."

"Why are you weeping, foolish girl," said I to her. "Am I reproaching you? Do I have any grievance against you? I'm in a dark and bitter mood, so I'm simply pouring out my heart, I'm talking to Him, to the Almighty, telling Him how He deals with me. He is a merciful Father, He pities me, but shows His power over me—He shouldn't punish me for my words—He settles accounts with me, and what can I do? Shout for help?"

I told her that probably things were meant to be so. He is up high above us, while we are down here, deep, deep in the ground, so we must say that He is right and His judgment is right, because if we look at it otherwise then I am nothing but a great fool. Why am I shouting, making such a racket? I am a tiny worm, I said, that wriggles down here on earth, so small that the slightest breeze, if God so wishes, could destroy me in an instant. Now do I have to make a stand with my foolish wits and try to tell Him how He should rule His little world? Probably, since He orders it to be so, it must be so; of what good are complaints? In our Holy Books it is written, said I, that forty days before a child is conceived in its mother's womb an angel comes along and announces: "The daughter of so-and-so will marry so-and-so!!" Let Tevye's daughter marry a Getzel, son of a Zorach, and Leizer-Wolf the butcher go elsewhere to find his mate; what is due to him won't run away, while you, said I, God should send your predestined one, only he should be a worthy man, and the sooner the better. Let His will be done, and I hope your mother doesn't yell too much, but I'll get enough from her anyhow!

Finally, we got home. I unharnessed the horse and then sat down on the grass near the house to try and think up what to tell my wife, to invent a tale from the *Arabian Nights,* so as to avoid trouble.

Evening was approaching. The sun was setting, frogs were croaking in the distance, the horse, hobbled, was munching grass, the cows, just returned from pasture, were standing over their mangers, waiting to be milked. All around me was the smell of grass—a true Garden of Eden! So I sat meditating and thinking how cleverly the Almighty had created this little world of His, so that each creature, from a human being to a cow, should earn its bread, nothing is for free! You, cow, if you wish to eat—let yourself be milked, yield milk, support a man and his wife and children. You, little horse, if you want to munch—trot back and forth to Boiberik, day in, day out, with the pots and crocks. The same goes for you, Man. If you want a piece of bread—go and toil, milk the cows, run around with the jugs and pitchers, churn butter, make cheese, harness the horse and drag yourself early every morning to Boiberik to the *dachas,* bow and scrape before the rich Yehupetzers, ingratiate yourself with them, smile at them, see to it that they are satisfied. God forbid you should injure their pride! Still, there remains the question: *"Mah nishtano?"* —where is it written that Tevye must slave for them, get up at the break of day, when God himself is still asleep, and for what? So that they should have fresh cheese and butter for their morning coffee? Where is it written that I must wear myself out working for a thin gruel, a *kulesh* of groats, while they, those rich Yehupetzers, rest their bones at their dachas, don't lift a finger for themselves and eat roast ducklings, good *knishes, blintzes* and *vertutti?* Am I not a Jew like they are? In all fairness, why shouldn't Tevye spend at least one summer at a *dacha?* Ah, but where will the cheese and butter come from? Who will milk the cows?.. Why, they, the Yehupetz rich, that's who!.. This crazy notion made me burst out laughing. As the saying goes, if God listened to fools, the world would have another face.

"Good evening, Reb Tevye!" someone greeted me. Turning around, I saw an acquaintance, Motl Kamzoil, a young tailor from Anatovka.

"Welcome! Mention the Messiah and see who comes!" said I. "Sit down, Motl, on God's good earth. What's brought you here all of a sudden?"

"What's brought me here? My feet!" he answered and sat down near me on the grass, looking towards the barn where my girls were flitting back and forth with the pots and jugs.

"It's already quite some time since I've wanted to come and see you, Reb Tevye," he said, "but I never seem to have the time: you finish one piece of work and take another. I now work for myself; there is, thank God, enough work, all of us tailors have as many orders as we can manage: it's been a summer of weddings. Berel Fonfach is having a wedding, Yosel Sheigetz is having a wedding, Mendel Zayika is having a wedding, Yankel Piskach is having a wedding, Moishe Gorgel is having a wedding, Meir Krapiva is having a wedding, Chaim Loshak is having a wedding and even the widow Trehubikha is getting ready for a wedding."

"The whole world," said I, "is celebrating weddings, I am the only exception; apparently, I am not worthy in God's eyes."

"No," said he, looking towards the place where the girls were. "You are mistaken, Reb Tevye. If you wished, you could also be getting ready for a wedding, it depends only on you..."

"How come?" I asked. "Maybe you mean a match for my Tzeitl?"

"A perfect fit!"

"Is it at least a worthy match?" I asked, thinking meanwhile: won't it be a fine thing if he means Leizer-Wolf the butcher!

"Cut and sewn to measure!" he retorted in tailors' talk, still looking off to where the girls were.

"From where, for instance," I asked him, "is this match of yours, from what parts? If he smells of a butcher shop I want to hear and see nothing of him!"

"God forbid," he answered, "by no means does he even begin to smell of a butcher shop. You know him very well, Reb Tevye!"

"Is this really a straight thing?" I asked.

"And how," said he, "straight! Straighter than straight! It is, as they say, merry, cheerful and lively—cut just right and sewn expertly!"

"So who is the man, tell me?" I asked.

"Who is the man?" repeated Motl, his eyes still on the barn. "The man is, Reb Tevye... you must understand—it is I myself."

No sooner had he said these words than I jumped to my feet as if scalded, and he after me, and so we stood face to face like ruffled-up roosters.

"Either you've gone crazy, or just simply lost your mind! You are the matchmaker, the in-law and the bridegroom all in one, that is, a whole wedding with your own musicians! I've never," said I, "heard anywhere that a young man should be his own matchmaker!"

"As regards what you say, Reb Tevye, about me being crazy—let all our enemies go crazy. I still have, you may believe me, all my wits about me. One doesn't have to be crazy to want to marry your Tzeitl. For example, Leizer-Wolf, who is the richest man in our town, also wanted to take her, even without a dowry...Do you think it's a secret? The whole *shtetl* already knows it! And as for your saying that I have come alone, without a matchmaker—you simply amaze me, Reb Tevye! After all, you are a man who knows something of the world. But why beat about the bush? This is the story: your daughter Tzeitl and I pledged our troth more than a year ago."

If someone had stabbed me to the heart I would have felt much better than when I heard these words: first of all, how comes he, Motl the Tailor, to be Tevye's son-in-law? Secondly, what kind of talk is this: they had pledged their troth, given each other their word to marry? And what about me? So I said to him:

"Cut and sewn to measure!" he retorted in tailor's talk.

"Don't I have some say where it concerns my child, or nobody asks me at all?"

"God forbid!" cried Motl. "that's just the reason why I came to have a talk with you, for I heard that Leizer-Wolf had proposed a match, and I have loved your daughter for over a year already."

"So if Tevye has a daughter named Tzeitl and your name is Motl Kamzoil and you are a tailor, then what can you have against her that you should dislike her?" I asked.

"No," said he, "that's not what I mean, I mean an altogether different thing. I wanted to tell you that I have been in love with your daughter for more than a year and that your daughter loves me and that we have pledged our word to each other to marry. I've wanted to come and talk the matter over with you several times, but have been putting it off for later, until I lay a few rubles aside to buy a sewing machine, and after that get myself decently clothed, since nowadays any self-respecting young man has to have two suits and several good shirts."

"Oh, get lost with your childish reasoning!" I shouted at him. "What will you do after the wedding, throw your teeth up into the rafters, or maybe feed your wife with shirts?"

"Eh, I really am surprised at you, Reb Tevye, that you should say such things! I mean, it seems to me that when you got married you owned no brick mansion, and yet... One thing or another—whatever happens to the Children of Israel will happen to Reb Israel. After all, I am a bit of a craftsman, too."

To make a long story short—he talked me into giving my consent. After all, why kid ourselves—how do all Jewish children get married? If one were to look at these things too closely, people of our class would never get married at all.

Only one thing troubled me, and I couldn't for the life of me understand it: what did it mean—they had given their word to each other? They themselves! What has the world come to? A boy meets a girl and says to her: "Let's get engaged, give each other our word to get married." That's simply wanton behavior!

However, when I took a look at my Motl, as he stood there with his head bowed, like a sinner, I saw that he was in full earnest, not trying any trickery, and then I had second thoughts. Let's look at the matter in another way. Why am I putting on such airs? Am I of such noble descent—Reb Tzotsele's grandson—or am I giving my daughter such a great dowry, or a splendid outfit? Alas! Yes, Motl Kamzoil is really a tailor, but he is a fine young man, hard-working, can earn his wife's bread, and an honest boy, too, so what have I against him? Tevye, I told myself, raise no foolish objections, and say, as it is written in the Good Book: *"I have forgiven you"*—I wish you happiness!

Yes, but what's to be done about my old woman? She'll make such a scene! How can I reconcile her to this match?

"You know what, Motl?" I said to the young suitor, "You go back home, I'll fix up things here meanwhile, have a talk with this one, that one. As it is written in The Book of Esther, *'The drinking was according to law'*—everything must be considered. And tomorrow, God willing, if you haven't changed your mind, we'll probably see each other."

"Change my mind?" he shouted. "Me change my mind? I shouldn't live to leave this spot, I should turn into a stone, a bone!"

"What's the use of swearing to me," said I, "when I believe you without your oath? Go in good health, and a good night to you, and may you have pleasant dreams."

I went to bed, too, but sleep wouldn't come; my head was almost splitting as I devised one plan after another, until at last I hit on the right one. What was this plan? Listen and you'll hear what Tevye can think up!

Around midnight, when the whole house was fast asleep, one snoring, another whistling, I suddenly started yelling at the top of my voice: "Help! Help! Help!!!" Naturally, my screams woke the whole family, first of all—Golda...

"God be with you, Tevye," she says, shaking me, "wake up, what's going on, why are you screaming?"

I open my eyes, pretend to be looking around on all sides, and exclaim, as if terrified: "Where is she?"

"Where is who—whom are you looking for?"

"Frumeh-Soreh," I answer, "Frumeh-Soreh, Leizer-Wolf's wife, was standing here just now..."

"You must be out of your head with a fever, Tevye, God save you!" exclaims my wife. "Leizer-Wolf's Frumeh-Soreh, may she rest in peace, passed over to the other world long ago."

"Yes," say I, "I know that she died, but still she stood right here just now by my bed and spoke to me, she grasped me by the throat and wanted to strangle me!

"God save you. Tevye, what are you babbling about?" says my

wife. "You saw a dream—spit three times and tell me the dream, and I'll interpret it for you as a good omen."

Long may you live, Golda," say I, "for having woken me up, otherwise I might have died on the spot from fright. Give me a drink of water and I'll tell you my dream. Only I must implore you, Golda, not to be frightened and think God knows what, because it stands written in our Holy Books that only three parts of a dream may sometimes come true, while all the rest is nonsense, falsehood...

"First of all," I said, "I dreamed that we were having a celebration, I don't know whether it was a betrothal party or a wedding. There were many people, both men and women, the rabbi and the *shokhet,* and musicians, too... Meanwhile, the door opens and in comes your Grandmother Tzeitl, may she rest in peace..."

Upon hearing about Grandmother Tzeitl, my wife went pale as a sheet and cried:

"What was her face like and what was she wearing?!"

"A face she had," I said, "I would wish on all our enemies, yellow as wax, and she was wearing, naturally, a white shroud. *'Mazl-tov! Mazl-tov!'* she said to me. 'I am happy that you have chosen for your Tzeitl, who carries my name, such a fine and decent bridegroom, his name is Motl Kamzoil. He was named after my Uncle Mordecai, and although he is a tailor, he is an honest boy...'"

"Where does a tailor come into our family?" asked Golda. "There are *melameds* in our family, cantors, blacksmiths, gravediggers, and just poor people, but, God forbid, nary a tailor nor cobbler!"

"Don't you interrupt me, Golda," said I, "probably your Grandmother Tzeitl knows better than you do... Upon hearing such congratulations from Grandmother Tzeitl, I said to her: 'Why do you say, Granny, that Tzeitl's betrothed is called Motl and that he is a tailor when actually his name is Leizer-Wolf and he is a butcher?'

"'Oh, no,' said Grandmother Tzeitl once more, 'no, Tevye, your Tzeitl's bridegroom is Motl, he is a tailor and with him she'll live to a ripe old age, God willing, in honor and riches...'

"'All right, Granny,' said I to her, 'but what is to be done about Leizer-Wolf? I gave him my word only yesterday!..'

"No sooner had I uttered these last words than Grandmother

61

Tzeitl vanished and in her place there appeared Leizer-Wolf's Frumeh-Soreh and addressed me in the following manner: 'Reb Tevye! I have always held you to be an honest man, a learned and virtuous man. But how comes it,' said she, 'that you should do such a thing, that you should want your daughter Tzeitl to be my heiress, to live in my house, keep my keys, put on my coat, wear my jewelry, my pearls?'

"'It isn't my fault,' said I, 'your Leizer-Wolf wanted it that way...'

"'Leizer-Wolf?' she screamed. 'Leizer-Wolf will come to a bad end, and your Tzeitl... A pity, Reb Tevye, on your daughter; she won't live with him for more than three weeks, I'll come to her at night and take her by the throat like this...' And with these words she began to strangle me, so that if you hadn't woken me up I would already have been far, far away..."

"Tfu, tfu, tfu!" spat out my wife three times. "May it fall into the river, may it sink into the earth, may it crawl into attics, may it rest in the forest, but it shouldn't harm us and our children! A wild and evil dream, may it fall on the butcher's head and on his hands and feet! He isn't worth Motl Kamzoil's littlest fingernail, even though Motl is a tailor, because if he was named after Uncle Mordecai he is most certainly not a born tailor. And since Grandmother, may she rest in peace, has taken the trouble to come back from the other world to congratulate us, we must say that this is probably for the best and it is just as it should be, in a lucky hour. *Amen Selah!*"

To make a long story short I tell you that I must have been stronger than iron that night if I didn't die of laughter lying there under my blanket... *"Praised by He who did not create me a woman"*—a woman is always a woman...

Next day, of course, we celebrated their betrothal, and soon after that, the wedding—almost at one stroke. The young couple now live quite contentedly: he plies his trade, goes around in Boiberik from *dacha* to *dacha* picking up work, she is busy day and night with the cooking and baking, washing and cleaning and fetching water from the well, and they barely make enough for bread; if I didn't bring them some dairy food from time to time, or a few *groszy,* things wouldn't have been at all good; but go talk to her; she says—knock on wood—that she is as happy as can be, only her Motl should be in good health.

So go and argue with today's children! It's like I told you at the beginning—*"I have raised children."* You work your fingers to the bone for them, bash your head against the wall, but *"they haven't obeyed me"*—they insist that they know better. No, say what you will, but today's children are too clever!

But I'm afraid I've tried your patience this time more than ever before. Don't hold it against me, live in good health always.

1899

"Before I knew it, I found myself lying on the ground amidst all the empty crocks and pots, and the wagon on top of me."

Hodel

You are surprised, Mr. Sholom Aleichem, that Tevye hasn't been seen in such a long time? You say he has greatly changed, his hair has gone gray? Why, if you only knew what troubles, what heartache this Tevye has been having lately! As it is written: *"Man is born of dust, and to dust he returneth"*—man is weaker than a fly and stronger than iron... A real character out of a book, that's me! Wherever some pestilence, some misfortune or trouble crops up— it never dares miss me! Why is this so, can you tell me? Maybe it is because I am a trusting person and take everyone at his word? Tevye forgets what our wise men have warned us of thousands of times: *"Believe him but keep an eye on him,"* which in plain language means: "Don't trust a dog." But what can I do, I ask you, if such is my nature?

As you know, I am a great optimist and never lodge any complaints with the Eternal One. Whatever He ordains is good—for even if one did try to complain, would it be of any use? Since we say: *"My soul is for Thee and my body is Thine,"* then what does man know and what is he worth? I always argue with her, with my old woman: "Golda," I say, "you're sinning! We have a *midrash*..."

"What's your *midrash* to me," she says, "we have a daughter of a marriageable age, and after this daughter there come, knock on wood, another two daughters, and after these two—another one, let no evil eye fall on them!"

"Pshaw, Golda, that's nonsense," say I. "This, too, was foreseen by our wise men. There's a *midrash* for this that says..."

But she won't let me talk: "Daughters, grownup daughters, are of themselves a good *midrash!*" Go argue with a woman!

So you see that I have, knock on wood, a choice of merchandise, real good wares, I can't complain—one girl is prettier than the other. It isn't for me to praise my own children, but I hear what the world says: "Beauties!" And the prettiest is the second one, Hodel

64

is her name, she is next after Tzeitl, the one who fell in love with a tailor, if you remember, and so cooked her own goose. As for looks—this second daughter of mine, Hodel, I mean—what shall I say? She is, as it is written in our sacred Book of Esther, *"of beautiful form and fair to look upon"*—shines like gold! Besides, as bad luck would have it, she has to have a head, too, reads and writes Yiddish and Russian, and as for books—she swallows them whole! You may well ask: what is there in common between Tevye's daughter and books, when her father deals in cheese and butter? That's just what I ask them, the fine young men, I mean, who haven't got a pair of pants, begging your pardon, they can call their own, but they have an urge to study. As we say in the *Haggadah:* *"We are all sages"*—everybody wants to learn, everybody wants to study. Go ask them: study what? Why? Goats should know as much about jumping into a neighbor's garden! Why, they aren't even permitted to enroll anywhere! Hands off!—shoo, away from the butter, kitty!

But you should see *how* they study! And who? Children of workmen—of tailors, of cobblers—so help me God!

Off they go to Yehupetz, or to Odessa, "lodge" in garrets, eat plagues and wash them down with fevers, for months on end don't as much as look a piece of meat in the eye, six of them pool their money to buy one loaf and a herring and—heigh-ho, make merry, paupers!...

In short, one such boy landed in our corner of the world, not far from here; I used to know his father, he was a cigarette-maker, as poor as poor can be. If our great sage Reb Jochanan Hasendler was not ashamed to sew boots, there is nothing wrong with having a father who rolls cigarettes.

One thing, however, troubles me: why should a poor man be so anxious to learn, to study? True, the devil didn't catch him, he has a good head on his shoulders, a very good head. His name is Perchik—"little pepper," but we translated it into Yiddish as Feferl—peppercorn. He really does look like a pepper, you should see him: a wizened, black and homely creature, but chock-full of brains, and with a tongue—real brimstone!

Well, here is what happened one day as I was driving home from Boiberik. I'd sold my wares, a full transport of cheese and butter and cream and various greens. Sitting in my wagon I lost myself, as I often do, in thoughts of heavenly things, of this and that, of the rich people from Yehupetz who had it so good, knock on wood, so good, and of Tevye the *shlimazl* and his little horse who both slaved throughout life, and so on.

It was summertime, the sun was hot, the flies were biting, and the world all around me was a delight, vast and open. I felt like getting up and flying, or stretching out and swimming!..

Meanwhile, I looked around and saw a lad striding on foot through the sand, carrying a bundle under his arm, sweating and out of breath.

"'*Rise, Yokel, son of Flekel!*'" I cried to him. "Here, come along, I'll give you a lift, my wagon is empty. How is it written in our Book? *If you see the ass belonging to a friend of yours lying under its burden you shall not pass it by*—all the more so a human being." So he laughs and climbs into my wagon.

"From where, for instance," I ask him, "does a young man pace?"

"From Yehupetz."

"What had a lad like you to do in Yehupetz?"

"A lad like me is taking examinations."

"And what profession," I ask, "may a lad like you be studying for?"

"A lad like me," he says, "isn't sure himself yet what he is studying for."

"If that is the case," say I, "why does a lad like you trouble his head in vain?"

"Don't you worry, Reb Tevye," retorts he, "such a lad as I knows what he is doing."

"Since you know who *I* am," I say, "then why not tell me, for instance, who *you* are?"

"Who am I? I am a human being."

"I see," say I, "that you're not a horse! I mean, *whose* are you?"

"Whose should I be? I am God's."

"That I know—that you are God's" I say. "It is written in our Books, *All living things are His.*' what I mean is from whom do you stem; are you one of ours, or maybe from Lithuania?"

"I *stem,*" says he, "from our forefather Adam, but I *come* from this neighborhood, you know me."

"So who is your father, come on, tell me!"

"My father," says he, "was called Perchik."

"Phoo," I spit in annoyance, "did you have to torture me so long? So you are the son of Perchik the cigarette-maker?"

"So I am the son of Perchik the cigarette-maker," he admits.

"And you study," I say, "in the 'classes'?"

"And I study," says he, "in the 'classes'."

"All right," say I, *Adam* is a man and *'tzipur'* is a bird, but tell me, my jewel, what, for instance, do you live on?"

"I live on what I eat."

"Aha," say I, "that's good; so what do you eat?"

"Anything I can get."

"I understand, you're not finicky: if there is something to eat you eat, if not—you bite your lip and go to bed hungry. But this is all worthwhile—as long as you can study in your 'classes'. You think you're equal to the rich boys of Yehupetz? As the verse goes: *'All are beloved, all are chosen.'*"

And I went on talking to him in this manner, giving him chapter and verse.

But you have another guess coming if you think he listened meekly: "They won't live to see the day I equal myself with them, those rich Yehupetz brats! To hell with them!"

"It seems to me that you really have it in for those rich people! I'm afraid they must have divided your father's inheritance among themselves!"

"Let me tell you that I and you and all of us possibly have a large share in *their* inheritance," said he.

"You know what—let your enemies speak for you. I notice only one thing: you are not a pampered young man and your tongue needs no sharpening; if you have the time, come over to my house this evening, we'll talk a little and you'll have supper with us."

Of course, I didn't have to repeat my invitation; he arrived in the evening, right on the dot—when the borsht was already on the table and the dairy *knishes* were frying in the oven.

"If you wish," I said to him, "wash your hands and say grace, if not—you can eat unwashed—I'm not God's steward, I won't be beaten in the other world for your sins."

As I talked to him I felt that somehow I was attracted to this little man; just what it was I don't know myself, but drawn to him I was. I like people with whom one can exchange a few words, sometimes a proverb, sometimes a *midrash,* or discuss heavenly things, this, that, and another—that's the kind of person Tevye is.

From that day on my young man began to drop in almost

every evening. He had a few private pupils, so as soon as he had finished with his lessons, he would come over to me to relax and enjoy himself a little. You can imagine what he got for his lessons if our wealthiest man is used to paying no more than three rubles a month, and the teacher has to, moreover, help him with his paper-work—read telegrams, write addressees and even run errands sometimes. And why not? As it is written: *"With heart and soul"*—if you eat bread you should know for what. He was lucky, though, that he ate with us most of the time, and for this he gave lessons to my daughters; as the Book says: *"Eye for eye"*—a slap for a slap.

In this manner he became like a member of our family. The children would ply him with glasses of milk, while my old woman took care that he should always have a clean shirt and a pair of darned socks. That was when we changed his name to Feferl—the Yiddish word for the Russian *perchik;* it may truly be said that the whole family came to love him as if he were our own kin, for by nature, I'll let you know, he is really a fine person, nothing under-hand about him: *"Mine is yours, yours is mine."*

There was only one thing I didn't like about him: his disap-pearances. All of a sudden he would up and go, and—*"The child vanished"*—no more Feferl! "Where have you been, my dear song-bird?" He's as mute as a fish.

I don't know about you, but I hate a person with secrets. What I like is, as they say, to *talk* and to *tell.* But one must give him his due: once he did start talking it was *"who by fire, who by water will be destroyed"*—fire and water! What a tongue—Heaven preserve us! He spoke *"against the Lord and against His anointed, let us break their bands asunder."* The most important thing, of course, was breaking the bands. Such wild ideas he had, absurd, crazy plans, everything topsy-turvy, upside-down! For instance, a rich man, according to his crazy notions, is worthless, while a poor man, quite the opposite, is the real goods, and if he is a workman he tops the stack, because he works with his own hands, and that's what is most important.

"Still," I said, "that doesn't come up to money."

This made him furious and he tried to convince me that money was the root of all evil on earth. Money, he said, is the source of all the falseness in the world, and everything that goes on is not fair, and because of money injustice reigns over the world. And he cited me thousands of arguments and examples that made no sense to me at all...

"It comes out," I said, "that, according to your crazy reasoning, the fact that my cow is milked and my horse draws loads is also not fair?" Such and other tricky questions I asked him, bringing him up short at every step, as Tevye can! But my Feferl also knows how to argue—and does he know! I wish God hadn't granted him such skill!

If Feferl had anything on his heart he immediately came out with it. We were sitting outside my house one evening, discussing all the aspects of these matters—it's called philosophy. Suddenly he remarked, Feferl, that is: "You know what, Reb Tevye? You have very bright daughters!"

"Really, I thank you for the news, they have whom to take after," was my retort.

"One of them," he went on. "the eldest one, is very sensible, a human being in the full sense of the word."

"That I know without your telling me," said I, "the fruit doesn't fall far from the tree."

That's what I said to him, but my heart, naturally, melted with pleasure, for what father, I ask you, doesn't like to hear his children praised? How was I to foresee that this praise would grow into a fiery emotion, Heaven protect us?

Well, *"And it was night and it became day"*—the time was between day and night. I was driving along in Boiberik from *dacha* to *dacha* when somebody stopped me. I took a look—it was Ephraim the Matchmaker. This Ephraim, you must know, is a matchmaker like any other matchmaker; that is, he arranges matches. Upon seeing me in Boiberik he, Ephraim I mean, stopped me, saying:

"Excuse me, Reb Tevye, there is something I have to tell you."

"My pleasure, only let it be a good thing," I said and stopped my horse.

"You, Reb Tevye, have a daughter!" he said.

"I have," said I, "seven daughters, God bless them."

"I know," said he, "that you have seven; I have seven myself."

"So we have," said I, "a total of fourteen daughters."

"All right," he went on, "let's finish with the joking. What I have to tell you is this: I am, as you know, a matchmaker, and I have a match for you, a young man who is something special from special-land! Top quality!"

"And what," asked I, "do you call something special, top quality? If he is a tailor, a cobbler, or a *melamed,* then let him stay where he

"And for this he gave lessons to my daughters."

is, and for me, as it is written, *freedom and deliverance will come from another*'—I'll find my equal somewhere else, as the *Midrash* says."

"Eh, Reb Tevye, you're starting on your *midrashim*? Before talking with you one has to tighten his belt! You shower the world with *midrashim*. Better hear out what a match Ephraim the Matchmaker wants to offer you; you just listen and keep quiet." And with this he began to read me his bill of sale.

What can I say? Something really out of the ordinary. In the first place, he comes from a good family, he's no upstart without kith or kin; this, you should know, is the main thing for me, since I am no nobody myself: in my family there are all kinds of people—*"spotted, striped, and speckled,"* as it stands in the Bible; we have just plain people, we have workers and we have men of property... Then, the young man is a scholar who is well-versed in the fine little letters. With me this is no small matter because I hate an ignoramus as I hate pork! To me an unlettered man is a thousand times worse than a rowdy; as far as I'm concerned you may go around without a cap, or even upside-down, but if you know what Rashi says you are already one of mine! That's the kind of person Tevye is!

"Then," went on Ephraim, "this man is rich, chock-full of money, he drives in a carriage drawn by a pair of fiery steeds—you even see the smoke!"

Well, thought I to myself, that isn't a bad thing, either. Better a rich man than a pauper. As it is written: *"Poverty is fitting for Israel."* God himself hates a pauper, otherwise a poor man wouldn't be poor.

"Well," asked I, "what else?"

"What else? He wants to become related to you—he's so eager, he's almost dead! That is, it's not exactly you he has in mind, he's dying to marry your daughter, he wants to marry a beauty, that's what he wants...."

"Oh, that's the way it is?" said I. "Let him go on wanting. But who is he, this rarity of yours—a bachelor, a widower, a divorcee, a black year?"

"He is a bachelor," said Ephraim, "although not so young, but a bachelor."

"And what," I asked, "is his holy name?"

That the matchmaker wouldn't tell me, go take and roast him alive!

"Bring her," said he, "to Boiberik, then I'll tell you."

"What do you mean—I should bring her? You can bring a horse to the fair, or a cow to be sold!"

Well, matchmakers, you know, can persuade a wall. We fixed a date: after next Saturday I would bring her, God willing, to Boiberik.

All kind of sweet thoughts came into my mind. I already imagined my Hodel driving in a carriage drawn by a pair of fiery steeds, and the whole world envying me, not so much because of the carriage and horses, as because of the benefits I bring the world through my rich daughter; I help the fallen with loans through my rich daughter; I help the fallen with loans without interest—I let this one have twenty-five rubles, that one fifty, another one a hundred; as you say, other people have souls, too.

So I meditated, driving home towards evening, giving the horse the whip and talking horse-language: "Horsie," I said, "giddy-up, giddy-up, hey, now just make with the legs a little faster, then you'll get your portion of oats sooner; as the Bible says: *'Without food there's no learning'*—if you don't grease the axles the wheels won't turn."

As I was talking in this manner to my horse I noticed two people coming out of the woods—a man and a woman, apparently. They were walking close to each other, talking very earnestly. Who could they be, I thought as I peered at them through the fiery rays of the setting sun. I could swear that it was Feferl! With whom was he strolling, the *shlimazl,* so late? I shielded my eyes with my hand and looked closer: who was the female? Eh, doesn't she look like Hodel? Yes indeed, as I live—it's Hodel! So this is how they study grammar and read books? Oh, Tevye, aren't you a fool! With such thoughts I stopped my horse and called out to the young people:

"A good evening to you, and what's the latest news about war? How come you're here all of a sudden? Whom are you waiting for? The day that's gone by?"

Upon hearing such a greeting my young couple stopped— *"Neither in Heaven nor on Earth"*—which means neither here nor there, shamefaced and blushing.

They stood so for a few minutes without uttering a word, their eyes downcast; then they raised their eyes and began to look at me, and I at them, and they at each other.

"Well," said I, "you're looking at me as if you hadn't seen me for a long time. It seems to me that I'm the selfsame Tevye as before. Not changed a hair."

72

I spoke to them half in anger, half in jest. At last my daughter Hodel, her face redder than before, said:

"Father, we should be congratulated."

"*Mazl-tov* to you," said I, "with good luck may you live. What's the celebration? Did you find a treasure in the woods? Or maybe you've just had a narrow escape from a great danger?"

"We should be congratulated," said Feferl, "we are betrothed."

"What do you mean," asked I, "by 'betrothed'?"

"Don't you know what 'betrothed' means?" he asked. "Betrothed means that I am engaged to marry her and she is engaged to marry me."

Speaking so, Feferl looked right into my eyes. But I also looked straight into *his* eyes, and I said:

"When was your betrothal-party? Any why didn't you invite me to the joyous event? I'm something of a relative, am I not?"

You understand, I joked with them, but worms were eating me, preying on my soul. But no matter, Tevye is not a woman, Tevye likes to hear out things to the end...

"I don't understand," said I, "a match without a matchmaker, without a marriage contract?"

"What do we need matchmakers for?" he, Feferl, asked. "We've been engaged for a long time already."

"Really? Divine miracles! So why did you keep quiet about it until now?"

"Why should we shout?" he asked. "We wouldn't have told you today, either, if not for the fact that we'll soon be parting, so we've decided that before this happens we must get married..."

This, as you understand, upset me greatly. *"The water reached up to the neck"*—I was hurt to the quick. His saying that they were engaged—well, that I could endure—how is it written? *"A'ave"*—love—he wants her, she wants him. But marriage? What words, "We must get married!" Gibberish!

It seemed that the bridegroom-to-be understood that I'd become a bit unhinged, so he said:

"See, Reb Tevye, this is how things stand: I have to go away from here."

"When are you leaving?"

"Very soon."

"Where, for instance, are you going?"

"This," said he, " I can't tell you, it's a secret..."

You hear? It's a secret! How do you like that?! Along comes a

73

Feferl, a small, dark, homely creature, presents himself as a bridegroom, wants to marry my daughter, is about to leave and won't say where to! Isn't it galling!?

"All right, a secret is a secret," said I; "everything is a secret with you. Only let me understand this, brother: you, after all, are a man of honor and are immersed in humaneness from head to toe. So how does it figure with you that you should all of a sudden out of the blue, take Tevye's daughter and turn her into a grass widow? This is what you call honor? Humaneness? I'm lucky that you haven't robbed me or set my house on fire..."

"Father!" exclaimed my daughter Hodel, "you just can't imagine how happy we are, he and I, that we've let out our secret to you. It's a load off our hearts. Come, Father, let's kiss each other."

Without more ado both of them embraced me, she on one side, he on the other, and they started kissing me and hugging me, and I them, and, evidently out of great zeal, the two of them began to kiss each other! A spectacle, I tell you, a real theater!

"Maybe it's already enough," said I, "of kissing? It's time to talk of practical matters."

"What practical matters?"

"A dowry," said I, "clothing, wedding expenses, this, that, and the other..."

"We need nothing," said they, "neither this, nor that, nor the other."

"Then what is it you do need?"

"We need," they said, "only the wedding ceremony."

Did you ever hear the like?

Well, in short, my words had as much weight with them as last year's snow, they had their wedding! Of course, you understand that it wasn't at all the sort of wedding that suited Tevye. What a wedding!.. A very quiet ceremony—woe is me!

Moreover, there was my wife, too—as one says, a blister on a boil! She nagged me, pestered me to tell her the reason for such a harum-scarum, hasty wedding. Go explain a fire to a woman! So I had to invent a maudlin story about an inheritance, a rich aunt in Yehupetz, all lies, all for the sake of peace.

On the same day, that is, a few hours after this fine wedding, I hitched up my horse and wagon and the three of us got in—that is, I myself, my daughter and he, the new-fledged son-in-law of mine, and we went to the railway station in Boiberik. Sitting in my wagon I glanced stealthily at the couple and thought to myself:

74

what a great God we have and how wondrously He rules this world of His! What strange, absurd beings He has created! Here you have a young couple just from under the wedding canopy: he is going away, the devil knows where, but she is staying behind—and not a single tear do you see, for appearance's sake at least! But no matter, Tevye is not a woman, Tevye has time, he can wait and see what the outcome will be...

Well, I saw a couple of young men, fine fellows with worn-out boots who came to the train to say goodbye to my song-bird. One of them was dressed like a peasant, I beg your pardon, with his shirt hanging out over his trousers; a whispered conversation took place between him and my son-in-law.

Look at that, Tevye, I said to myself, maybe you've gotten mixed up with a gang of horse-thieves, purse-snatchers, lock-breakers, or counterfeiters?..

Driving home from Boiberik with Hodel I couldn't keep these thoughts to myself. She burst out laughing and tried to convince me that these were very fine young men, honest, extremely honest, men whose entire lives were dedicated to the welfare of others, who didn't think of themselves at all.

"The one with the shirt," said she, "comes from a most respectable family, he left his wealthy parents in Yehupetz and won't take a broken *grosz* from them."

"Really? Actually a very fine young man, as I live!" said I. "In addition to the shirt hanging out over his pants and his long hair, if God should help him to acquire an accordion, or a dog to run after him—that, indeed, would be most extremely charming!"

With such talk I was getting even with her, and with him, too, pouring out the bitterness of my heart, that is, on the poor girl....

And she? Nothing! *"Esther held her peace."* Makes as if she doesn't understand.

I say: "Feferl." She comes out with: "For the common weal, workers..." A hopeless thing!

"What's the use," said I, "of your 'common weal' and your workers if everything is a secret with you? There is a proverb that says: Where there's a secret there's thievery... So tell me, daughter, why did he leave—Feferl, I mean—and where did he go?"

"Anything else," said she, "but not this. You'd better not ask about it. Believe me, when the time comes you'll know everything. God willing, you'll hear, and perhaps very soon, many things, much good news!"

"Amen," said I, "let it be from your lips to God's ear. But our enemies should know as much of health as I have even an inkling of what is going on here with you and what the play-acting means!"

"That's just the trouble—you won't understand."

"Why so? Is it so hard to understand? It seems to me that I understand more difficult things."

"This cannot be understood," said she, "with the mind alone. It must be felt, felt with the heart..."

That is how my daughter Hodel spoke to me, and while she talked, her face flamed and her eyes burned. Heaven preserve these daughters of mine! When they get involved in something, it's with mind and heart, with body and soul!

In short, I'll tell you that a week went by, two, three, four, five, six and seven weeks— *"Neither voice nor money"*—no letters, no messages.

"Feferl is lost!" As I said this, I glanced at my Hodel: there was not a drop of blood in her face, poor girl, and she went about the house looking for something to do, trying, apparently, to drown her grief in work. Still, she never even as much as mentioned his name! Hush, quiet, just as if there had never even been a Feferl in the world!

However, one day, when I came home, my Hodel's eyes were swollen from tears. I started to ask questions and found out that not long ago she had had a visitor—a long-haired *shlimazl*, who had spoken in secret to her. Aha, thought I, that must be the fellow who left his rich parents and wears his shirt over his pants... So without more ado I called my Hodel out into the yard and asked her bluntly:

"Tell me, daughter, have you already heard from him?"

"Yes."

"Where is he then, your predestined one?"

"He is," says she, "far away."

"What is he doing?"

"He's in prison!"

"In prison?"

"In prison."

"Where is he in prison? Why is he in prison?"

No answer. She looks me straight in the face and keeps quiet.

"Only tell me, daughter mine," said I, "as I understand, he is in prison not for robbery; in that case, since he is no thief and no swindler, I don't understand why he is in prison, for what good deeds?"

She was silent. *"Esther held her peace."* Well, thought I, you don't want to tell me—don't; he is your affliction, not mine. Serves him right! But inside, in my heart, I carried a pain. I am, after all, a father; doesn't it say in our prayers: *"As a father pities his children"*—a father is always a father.

Well, the evening of *Hashono Rabo* came. On a holiday it's my custom to take a rest, and my horse, too, rests. As the Torah says, *"Thou shalt rest from thy labors and so shall thy wife and thy ass..."* Besides, there is not much to do in Boiberik: it needs no more than one blow of the *shophar* to make all the *dachniki*, the summer people, scatter like mice during a famine, and Boiberik becomes a waste. At such times I like to be at home, to sit outdoors on the *prizba**. This is the best time for me. The days are gifts. The sun is no longer as hot as a lime kiln, it caresses you softly, a pleasure to the soul. The forest is still green, the pines still exude their pungent scent, and it seems to me that the forest takes on a festive look, that it is god's own tabernacle, his *sukkah;* this, I think, is where God celebrates *Sukkoth*—here, not in the cities where there is such a tumult, with people rushing back and forth, panting for breath, all for the sake of a piece of bread, and all one hears is money, money, and money!..

This night of *Hashono Rabo* was truly like Paradise: the sky was blue, the stars twinkled and blinked as if they were human eyes. Once in a while a star would shoot by, as an arrow flies from a bow, leaving for an instant a green streak—a falling star, somebody's luck had fallen. There are as many lucks as there are stars in the sky... Jewish luck... I hope it isn't my bad luck, was my thought, and this brought to mind Hodel. During the last few days she had become brighter, livelier, and looked altogether different. Somebody must have brought her a letter from him, from her *shlimazl*. I'd have liked to know what he wrote, but I didn't want to ask. She said nothing, so I kept quiet, too: Tevye is not a woman, Tevye can wait...

As I sat thinking about Hodel, she herself came out and sat down by my side on the *prizba*. Glancing around, she turned to me and said, in a low voice:

---

*A mound, or ledge, of earth banked against the outer walls of peasant houses (Ukrainian). — *Tr.*

"Do you hear, *Tateh?* I have to tell you something: today I am going to say goodbye to you... forever."

She said these words almost in a whisper, I could hardly hear her; her look was so strange—I'll never forget it. Meanwhile a thought flitted through my mind: She wants to drown herself!

Why did I think of drowning? Because—may this never happen to us—not long ago a Jewish girl, she lived not far from us, fell in love with a peasant boy and because of this boy... You understand already.... These troubles affected her mother so that she took sick and died, and her father spent everything he had and became a pauper. The peasant boy changed his mind and married somebody else. So she, the girl, I mean, went to the river, threw herself into the water and drowned...

"What do you mean," I asked, "that you are going to say goodbye forever?" As I spoke I looked at the ground, so that she shouldn't see how upset I was.

"It means," said she, "that early tomorrow morning I am going away and we'll never see each other again... Never..."

Upon hearing these words I felt a little better. Thank God for this at least—it might be worse, while better has no limit.

"Where, for instance are you going—if I might have the honor of knowing?" I asked.

"I'm going," said she, "to him."

"To him? So where is he now?"

"For the time being," she said, "he is still in prison; but soon he will be deported."

"So you're going, you mean, to say goodbye to him?" I asked, playing the fool.

"No," she answered, "I'm following him out there."

"Out there?.. Where is this 'out there,' what is the name of the place?"

"We don't know yet exactly what the place is called, but it is very far," she said, "far and full of terrible dangers."

That's what my Hodel told me, and it seemed to me that she spoke with elation, with great pride, just as if he'd accomplished something so important that he should be awarded a medal weighing at least thirty pounds!.. How was I to answer her? For such things a father gets angry with his child, hands out a couple of slaps or gives the child a good dressing down! However, Tevye is not a woman. To my way of thinking anger raises the devil. So I retorted, as I usually do, with a passage from the Bible:

"I see, my daughter, it is as the Bible says, *'Therefore shalt thou abandon...'* Because of a Feferl you're abandoning your father and mother and are going away to nobody knows where, somewhere out in a desolate place, on the shore, evidently, of the frozen sea where Alexander the Great sailed and got lost and was stranded on a distant island among savages, as I once read in a story-book..."

I spoke half in jest and half in anger, and all the time my heart wept. But Tevye is not a woman, Tevye restrains himself. Neither did she, Hodel, lose face: she answered me word for word, quietly, thoughtfully. Tevye's daughters can talk.

Although my head was bowed and my eyes were closed, yet it seemed to me that I saw her, Hodel, that is; I saw that her face was just like the moon, pale and lusterless, and her voice sounded muffled and it trembled... Should I fall on her neck, plead with her, implore her not to go? But I know that it won't help. Oh, these daughters of mine! If they fall in love, it's with soul and body, with heart and mind!

Well, we sat out there on the *prizba* for a long time, maybe all night. We were silent most of the time, and when we did speak it was almost not speech—half-words... She spoke and I spoke. I asked her only one thing: where did anyone hear of a girl marrying a fellow just in order to be able to follow him to the devil knows where!?

To this her answer was: "With *him* I don't care—I'll go anywhere, even to the devil knows where!"

I tried to explain to her how foolish this was. So she answered me that I would never be able to understand it. I told her a story about a hen that had hatched ducklings; no sooner did they gain the use of their legs than they took to the water, while the poor hen stood clucking on the shore.

"What," asked I, "will you say to that, daughter dear?'

"What," asked she, "can I say? It's a pity on the hen, but because the hen clucks should the ducklings not swim?.."

Can you understand such talk? Tevye's daughter utters no empty words...

Meanwhile time did not stand still. Dawn was already breaking. Inside the house my old woman grumbled. She had already sent for us several times, saying it was high time to go to bed; seeing that this was of no use, she stuck her head out of the window and said to me, with her usual benediction: "Tevye, what's got into you?!"

79

"In my heart I was like a boiling samovar, but I showed nothing."

"Let there be silence, Golda," said I, "as the Bible says, *"Why the uproar?.."* You must have forgotten that it is *Hashono Rabo* tonight? On *Hashono Rabo* our fates are sealed for the coming year, so on *Hashono Rabo* we stay up all night. Now you just do what I tell you, Golda: please kindle the fire in the samovar and let us have tea; meanwhile I'll go and hitch up the horse. I'm taking Hodel to the station."

And then, as my custom is, I made up a new cock-and-bull story about Hodel going to Yehupetz, and from there still further, all on account of that business, the legacy, and it might be that she would stay there over the winter, and maybe even over a winter and summer and another winter. Therefore, said I, we have to give her some food for the journey, some linen, a dress, a few pillows, pillowcases, this, that, and another.

As I ordered my womenfolk around, I told them there should be no weeping, for it was *Hashono Rabo.*

"There is an explicit law against weeping on *Hashono Rabo!*" I said.

Well, they minded me as a cat minds, and there was plenty of crying, and when the time of parting came there was such an uproar, such weeping—the mother, the children, and even she herself, Hodel, particularly when she was saying goodbye to my eldest daughter, Tzeitl. (She and her husband, Motl Kamzoil, always spend the holidays with us.) Both sisters fell on each other's necks—we could barely tear them apart...

I was the only one who didn't break down—I was as firm as steel and iron. I mean, that's just a saying, "steel and iron"; in my heart I was like a boiling samovar, but I showed nothing—fie! Tevye is, after all, not a woman!..

We didn't talk at all on the way to Boiberik, but when we were already near the station I asked her, for the last time, to tell me what, actually, he had done, her Feferl?

"Every thing," said I, "must have some sort of taste."

At this she flared up and swore by all the holiest oaths in the world that he was absolutely innocent of any crime, pure as fine gold.

"He is a man," she said, "who cares nothing about himself. All he did was for the good of others, for the good of the world, above all for the toilers, the working people..."—so be a sage and try to guess what that means!

"He worries about the world?" I asked her. "Then why doesn't

81

the world worry about him if he is such a fine fellow? But please give him my regards, this Alexander the Great of yours. Tell him that I rely on his honor, for he is a man of honor and I trust that he won't deceive my daughter and will write a letter once in a while to her old father..."

You think that as I spoke she didn't fall on my neck and begin to cry?

"Let us say goodbye," she said. "Farewell, *Tateh,* God knows when we will see each other again!"

At this I finally broke down myself... I remembered this very Hodel when she was a baby... a little child... I carried her in my arms... in my arms...

Please excuse me, Mr. Sholom Aleichem, that I... like an old woman... Oh, if you only knew what a daughter Hodel was... what a daughter... You should see the letters she writes... A godsend, this Hodel! She... deep, deep in my heart... deep, deep, I haven't the words to express what I feel...

You know what, Mr. Sholom Aleichem? Let us better talk of more cheerful things: what's the latest news about the cholera in Odessa?..

1904

Chava

"Give thanks to the Lord, for He is good"—whichever way God leads is good. That is, it should be good, for try and become a sage and make things better! Take me—I wanted to be clever, I interpreted Bible verses this way and that way and saw that it was of no use, so I gave it up as a hopeless job and told myself: Tevye, you're a fool! You won't overturn the world. The Almighty gave us *"the pain of bringing up children,"* which means the sorrows inflicted by children should be looked upon as blessings. For instance, my eldest daughter Tzeitl fell in love with the tailor Motl Kamzoil, so have I anything against him? True, he is a simple soul, not very well versed in the fine little letters, I mean, but what can be done? The whole world can't be educated, can it? But he is honest and hard-working, he works, poor man, by the sweat of his brow. They already have, you should only see, a houseful—knock on wood—of bare-bellied young ones, and both of them struggle *"in honor and in riches,"* as the saying goes. But talk with her, she'll tell you that everything is, knock on wood, fine with her, it can't be better. The only trouble is that there isn't enough food…There you have, so to say, round number one.

Well, and about the second daughter, I mean Hodel, I don't have to tell you, you already know. With her I gambled and lost, lost her forever! God alone knows whether my eyes will ever behold her again, unless we meet in the next world, in a hundred and twenty years... Whenever I speak of her, of Hodel, I still can't take it, it's the end of my life! Forget her, you say? How can one forget a living person? Especially such a child as Hodel? You should only see the letters she writes to me—your heart would melt! She writes that they are doing quite well out there. He sits in prison and she earns a living. She washes clothes and reads books and visits him every week; she hopes, she says, that the pot will boil over here, in our parts, the sun will rise and everything will brighten, and then he and many others like him will be released, and after that, she says, they will all begin their real work and turn the world upside-down. Well? How do you like that? Fine, isn't it?..

Yes, so what does the Almighty do? He is, after all, *"a gracious and merciful Lord,"* so He says to me: "Just you wait, Tevye, I will bring something to pass that'll make you forget all your former troubles..."

And sure enough—this is a story worth hearing. I wouldn't tell it to another person, because the pain is great and the shame is still greater! Only, as it is written in our Book: *"Shall I conceal it from Abraham?"*—I have no secrets from you. Whatever I have on my mind I tell you. But there is one request I want to make: let it remain between the two of us. I tell you once more: the pain is great, but the shame, the shame is still greater!

Well, as it stands in the *Perek: "The Holy One, blessed be He, wished to purify a soul"*—God decided to do Tevye a favor, so he went and blessed him with seven female children, daughters, that is, all of them lovely, clever, and beautiful, fresh and healthy—pine trees, I tell you! Oh, if only they had been ugly and ill-tempered it might have been better for them and healthier for me. Now, I ask you, what is the use of a good horse if it is kept in a stable? What's the good of having beautiful daughters when you're stuck away with them out in a hole where they see no live people except Ivan Poperilo, the headman of the village, or the clerk Fedka Galagan, a tall Gentile fellow with a mane of hair and high boots, and the Russian priest, may his name and his memory be blotted out. I just can't bear to hear his name—not because I am a Jew and he is a Christian priest. On the contrary, we have been well acquainted for many years. That is, we don't visit each other to have a talk, nor, of course, do we wish each other a happy holiday; but, no matter, when we meet we say good morning, a good year, what's new in the world? I hate to get involved in long conversations with him, because they are sure to turn into a discussion: your God, our God. But I don't let him go on—I interrupt with an aphorism and tell him that we have a certain verse in the Bible... So he interrupts me and says that he knows all these verses as well as I do, and perhaps even better, and he begins to recite our Holy Bible in Hebrew to me, with his Gentile pronunciation: *"Bereshit bara alokim"**—every time, every time the same thing. So I interrupt him again and

---

* *"In the beginning God created...",* the opening words of Genesis (Hebrew).—*Tr.*

tell him that we have a *Midrash...* "The *Midrash,*" he says, "is called the *Tal-mud,*" and he hates the *Tal-mud* for the *Tal-mud* is sheer trickery... So of course I get good and angry and start laying out anything that comes to my mind. Do you think he cares? Not at all! He looks at me and laughs, combing his beard with his fingers all the while. There is nothing more maddening in the world than the silence of a person you are shouting at, calling all manner of foul names—and not getting a word back! You are boiling, your bile is rising, while he just sits and smiles! At that time I couldn't understand it, but now I know what that smile meant...

Well, as I was coming home towards evening one day whom should I see standing near my house but the clerk Fedka, talking to my third daughter, Chava, the one who comes after Hodel. Upon seeing me the fellow about-faced, took off his cap to me and left. So I asked Chava:

"What was Fedka doing here?"

"Nothing," she answered.,

"What do you mean by nothing?" I asked.

"We were just talking."

"What's there for you to talk with Fedka about?"

"We've known each other for a long time."

"I congratulate you on your acquaintanceship! A wonderful friend—Fedka!" cried I.

"Do you know him then?" she asked. "Do you know who he is?"

"Who he is—that I don't know," said I, "I haven't seen his family register, however, I do understand that he probably stems from the greatest celebrities: his father must have been either a cowherd, or a watchman, or simply a drunkard."

To this she, Chava, that is, answered: "What his father was I don't know, to me all people are equal; but that he himself is no ordinary person—that I know for sure."

"And namely what sort of man may he be? Let me hear."

"I'd tell you," said she, "but you won't understand. Fedka—he is a second Gorky."

"A second Gorky? Then who was the first Gorky?"

"Gorky," she answered, "is almost the greatest man in the world today."

"Where does he live." I asked, "this sage of yours, what is his business and what kind of sermons does he preach?"

"Gorky," said my daughter, "is a famous writer, an author, a man who creates books, a wonderful, rare, honest person. He also comes from the common folk, he had no schooling at all but is self-educated. Here is his portrait," she said, taking a small picture out of a pocket and showing it to me.

"So this is he, your saintly man, Reb Gorky? I could swear that I've seen him somewhere," I said, "either at the railway station carrying sacks or in the woods hauling logs."

"So in your opinion," said she, "it's a fault if a man toiled with his own hands? Don't you yourself work hard? And don't we work hard?'

"Yes, yes," said I, "you are quite right. In our Law it says: *'When thou eatest the labor of thine own hands'*—if you don't work, you won't eat... Still, I cannot understand what Fedka was doing here. It would give me greater pleasure if you were acquainted with him at a distance; you mustn't forget *'Whence thou camest and whither thou goest'*—who you are and who he is."

Her answer to this was: "God created all men equal."

"Yes, yes, God created Adam our forefather in his own likeness, but we shouldn't forget that each one of us must seek his equal, as it is written: *'From each according to his means...'*"

"Amazing!" cried she. "For everything you have a quotation! Maybe you can also find one explaining why people divided themselves up into Jews and Gentiles, into lords and slaves, into nobility and beggars?"

"Tut-tut-tut, daughter!" said I. "It seems to me that you've gone too far — strayed, as they say, into the *'sixth millennium'.*"

I explained to her that this had been the way of the world since *"before the six days of Creation."*

So she asked: "Why should that be the way of the world?"

I answered: "Because that is how God created His world."

"Why did God create His world so?"

"Eh," said I, "if we started asking questions—why this and why that—*'there would be no end to it,'* it would be a tale without an end."

"God gave us reason," she said, "so that we should ask questions."

"We have a custom," said I, "that when a hen begins to crow like a rooster it is immediately taken to the slaughterer; as we say in the benediction: *'Who gave the rooster the ability to discern between day and night...'*"

"Maybe we've already had enough yammering out there?!"

86

shouted my Golda from the house. "The borsht," she said, "has been standing on the table for an hour already, but he's still singing Sabbath hymns!"

"Here we have another holiday!" said I. "It's not for nothing that our wise men said: *'Seven idle words hath a golem'*—a woman contains nine measures of speech. We're discussing important matters and she comes along with her milk borsht!"

"The milk borsht," said she, "may be just as important as all your 'important matters.'"

"Congratulations! Here we have a new philosopher, directly from under the oven! It isn't enough that my daughters have become enlightened—now Tevye's wife has begun to fly though the chimney up into the sky!"

"Talking of the sky," said Golda, "may the earth swallow you!"

How do you like, for example, such a welcome on an empty stomach?

To make it short, let us leave the prince and turn to the princess—I mean the priest, may his name and memory be forgotten!

One evening I was driving homeward with my empty jugs and crocks; just as I was coming into the village I met the priest coming from the opposite direction in his iron-coated britzka, proudly driving the horses himself, his well-combed beard flowing in the wind. May the ill luck from this encounter fall on your head, I thought to myself.

"Good evening!" said he. "Don't you recognize me, or what?"

"It's a sign that you'll soon become rich," said I to him, taking off my cap and intending to continue on my way.

"Wait a while, Tevel," said he. "What's the great hurry? I have a few words to say to you."

"Oh," said I, "if it's something good—very well, and if it isn't—keep it for another time."

"What do you mean by another time?" he asked.

"Another time means when the Messiah comes."

"But the Messiah," said he, "has come already."

"That I have heard from you before, and not once; better tell me, Father, something new."

"That's just what I mean to tell you," said he. "I want to have a talk with you about you yourself, that is, about your daughter."

This sent a pang through my heart: what had he to do with my daughter?

"My daughters," said I, "are, God forbid, not the kind of girls you have to speak for, they can stand up for themselves."

"But this," said he, "is a matter of which she herself cannot talk, another must speak for her, because it is a most important matter, her future depends on it."

"Whose concern is the future of my child?" I asked. "It seems to me that since we are speaking of futures I am a father to my child for a hundred and twenty years, isn't that so?"

"True," said he, "you are a father to your child. However, you are blind to her needs. Your child is reaching out for another world, but you don't understand her, or else you don't want to understand her!"

"Whether I don't understand her or don't want to understand her is another matter," said I. "This we can have a little talk about. But what has it got to do with you, Father?"

"It has quite a lot to do with me, for she is now under my care," he answered, looking me straight in the eye and combing his flowing beard with his fingers.

This jolted me, to be sure: "Who? My child is under *your* care? What right have you?" cried I, feeling my temper flaring up.

"Don't get so worked up, Tevel!" said he with a cold-blooded smile. "Slow down. You know that I am no enemy, God forbid, of yours, even though you are a Jew. You know that I respect Jews, that my heart bleeds for them, for their obstinacy, for their stubborn refusal to understand what is meant for their own good."

"Don't you talk to me of our own good, Father," said I, "for every word I now hear from you is like a drop of deadly poison, like a bullet piercing my heart. If you are, as you say, such a good friend of mine, I ask only one favor of you: leave my daughter alone..."

"You are a foolish man," he retorted. "Nothing bad, God forbid, will happen to your daughter. She will be happy—she is going to marry a fine man, I should live such a life."

"Amen!" said I, forcing myself to laugh, while my heart was a burning Gehenna. "And who may he be, this bridegroom, if I might have the honor of knowing?"

"You must know him" said the priest; "he is a fine and honest young man, and pretty well educated, although self-taught, and he loves your daughter and wants to marry her, but he can't, for he is not a Jew."

Fedka! was my instant thought, and I felt my head swimming;

a cold sweat broke out all over my body, I could barely keep my seat in the wagon. But I wouldn't let him see anything—he won't live to see the day! So I picked up the reins, gave the horse a few lashes and took off without a goodbye— *"departed like Moses."*

When I got home—oh, everything was topsy-turvy! The children were crying with their faces buried in pillows, weeping loudly, Golda was more dead than alive... I looked around for Chava—where is Chava? No Chava!

I knew better—woe is me—than to ask about her. I was beset by the torments of the grave, and a flame of anger burned in me, I don't know against whom... I felt like giving myself a beating... I started yelling at the children and let out the bitterness of my heart on my wife.

I couldn't find a place for myself, so I went out to the stall to feed the horse and found him standing with a leg twisted over the far side of his tough. I grabbed a stick and began laying into the poor beast as if bent on skinning him and breaking all his bones: "May you burn alive, *shlimazl!* May you starve to death—not a single oat grain will you get from me! Troubles, if you like, you may have, and anguish, blows and plagues!.."

Shouting so at the horse, I soon caught myself thinking: *A pity for living things"*—for a poor innocent beast—what do I have against him? I sifted a little chopped straw into the manger and promised the horse that I would show him, God willing, the letter "hay"* in my prayer-book on the Sabbath.

Then I went back into the house, lay down, and buried my head in the pillow. I felt as if my chest had been cut open, my head was splitting from thinking, from trying to understand, to grasp the real meaning of all this. *"How have I sinned and what is my transgression"*—how have I, Tevye, sinned more than the rest of the world that I am punished more than all the Jews? Oh, Almighty God, Lord of the Universe! *"Who are we and what is our life?"* Who am I that you always have me in mind, and never permit any blight, trouble or misfortune to pass me by?!

So ran my thoughts, and I felt as if I were lying on live coals; then I heard my poor wife groaning and sighing—my heart bled for her.

"Golda," I asked, "are you asleep?"

"No," she answered. "What then?"

---

*The name of the first letter of the word "hay" in Hebrew.—*Tr.*

"Nothing," said I, "we've got ourselves into a nice hole. Maybe you have some idea of what's to be done?"

"You ask me for advice," said she, "woe is me... A child gets up in the morning, strong and healthy, gets dressed and embraces me and begins to kiss me, hug me and bursts into tears, but says nothing. I thought that she—God forbid—had lost her mind! So I ask her: 'What's the matter with you, daughter?' She doesn't say a word and runs out into the yard to see to the cows and disappears. I wait an hour, I wait two hours, three hours—where is Chava? No Chava! So I tell the children to run over the priest's house for a minute..."

"How did you know, Golda, that she was there?"

"Alas and alack! Don't I have eyes? Or maybe I am not her mother?"

"If you have eyes and if you are her mother," said I, "then why didn't you say anything, why didn't you tell me?"

"Tell you? When are you at home? And when I do tell you something—do you listen to me? When a person tells you something you immediately answer with a quotation; you've drummed my head full of quotations and that's how you get by..."

That is what she, Golda, said to me, and I heard her weeping in the darkness... She is partly right, thought I, because what does a woman understand? It pained my heart to hear her groaning and weeping. So I said to her:

"Look, Golda, you are angry at me because I have a quotation for everything; well, even this I must answer with a quotation. It is written in our Book: *As a father has mercy on his children!*—a father loves his child. Why doesn't the passage read: *As a mother has mercy on her children*—that a mother loves her child? Because a mother is not a father; a father can speak differently to a child. Just wait, tomorrow, God willing, I'll see her."

"God grant," said she, "that you will be able to see her, and him, too. He is not a bad man, even though he is a priest; he does have compassion for people. You implore him, fall to his feet, perhaps he'll have mercy."

"Who, the priest, may his name be accursed!? I should stoop to the priest? Are you crazy or have you lost your mind? *Do not open your mouth to Satan,*'" said I, "my enemies won't live to hear of such things!"

"Ah, you see! There you go again!" exclaimed Golda.

"What did you think? That I should let myself be led by a woman? That I would live according to your female reason?"

90

We spent the whole night talking in this manner. At the first crow of the cock I got up, said my prayers, picked up my whip and set off straight for the priest's house. As you say, a woman is only a woman, but where else should I have gone? Into the grave?

When I entered the priest's yard his hounds gave me a splendid welcome and wanted to "fix" my cloak and taste the calves of my Jewish legs, to see whether they were good for their canine teeth... It was my good luck that I had taken my whip along; with its aid I made them understand the Hebrew quotation, *"Not a dog shall bark"*—or, as it goes in Ukrainian, *Nekhai sobaka darom nye breshet*—don't let a dog bark in vain.

The barking and the uproar brought the priest and his wife out into the yard. With difficulty they managed to drive off the merry pack, and then they invited me into the house, receiving me as an honored guest—they even wanted to put on the samovar for me. I said that the samovar was not necessary, that I had something I wanted to talk about with the priest eye-to-eye. He guessed what I meant and winked at his spouse to please shut the door from the other side.

I came straight to the point without any preamble: let him first tell me whether he believed in God... Then let him tell me whether he felt what it meant to part a father from a child he loved. Next, let him tell me what, to his mind, was a good deed and what was a sin? And another thing I wanted him to make clear to me: what does he think of a man who sneaks into another man's house and wants to change everything in it—move the chairs, the tables and beds?

Of course he was bewildered: "Tevel, you are a clever man, and here you come and hurl so many questions at me at once, and you want me to answer them all at one go. Wait a while and I'll answer all your questions, from first to last."

"No," said I, "my dear Father, you'll never answer these questions. Do you know why? Because I know all your thoughts beforehand. Better give me an answer to this: May I still hope to see my child again or not?"

At this he jumped to his feet: "What do you mean—see her again? Nothing will happen to your daughter, quite the opposite!"

"I know," said I, "I know you want to make her happy! That's not what I'm speaking about. I want to know where my child is, and whether I can see her?"

"Anything you want," said he, "but that—no."

"*Tevel, you are a clever man, and here you come and hurl so many questions at me at once.*"

"That's the way to talk," said I, "short and sweet and right to the point! Goodbye now, and may God repay you many times over!"

When I got home I found my Golda lying in bed all bunched up like a ball of black thread; her eyes had already run out of tears. I said to her: "Get up, my wife, take off your shoes and let us sit down on the floor and mourn our child for seven days, as God has commanded. *'The Lord hath given and the Lord hath taken away.'* We are not the first and we are not the last. Let it seem to us that we never had any Chava, or that she has left us, like Hodel who went off beyond the *'mountains of darkness'* and God alone knows whether we will ever see her again…The Almighty is a merciful God, He knows what He does!…"

With such talk I poured out the bitterness of my heart, feeling that tears were choking me, like a bone struck in my throat. But Tevye is not a woman, Tevye can restrain himself! That, of course, is only in a manner of speaking, because, first of all—the shame! And secondly, how can I restrain myself when I've lost a living child, especially such a child, a diamond embedded deep in both my own and her mother's hearts, almost more precious to us than all the other children, I don't know why. Perhaps it is because she had been very sickly as a little child, had suffered *"all the troubles of the world."* We used to sit up with her whole nights, several times we snatched her, literally snatched, out of the clutches of death, breathed life into her, as one would breathe on a tiny, trampled chick, because if God so wishes He makes the dead come to life again, as we say in a *hallel: "I shall not die but I shall live"*—if it is not ordained that you should die, you don't die…And maybe it is because she was a good and faithful child, she always loved us both with all her heart and soul. So I ask: how could it happen that she should cause us such grief? The answer is that, firstly, such was our luck. I don't know about you, but I believe in Providence; and secondly, it was some kind of witchcraft! You may laugh at me, but I must tell you that I am not so benightedly foolish as to believe in gnomes, elves, *domoviks**, spooks and other such nonsense. But I do believe in witchcraft, for what could it have been but witchcraft? Just hear me out and you will also say the same thing….

In short, as our Holy Books say, *"Perforce you must live"*—a

---

*A goblin, or brownie that was, according to superstition, supposed to live in every house (from the Russian word *dom*—house). — *Tr.*

human being does not take his own life—these are no idle words. There are no wounds that don't heal, and no trouble that is not forgotten with time. That is, one doesn't actually forget, but what can be done? *"Man is likened to a beast"*—a man must toil, suffer, labor to exhaustion for his piece of bread. So all of us got down to work, my wife and the children with the jugs and jars, I with my horse and wagon, and *"the world continued in its course"*—the world does not stand still. I told my family that Chava was *"never to be mentioned nor thought of"*—no more Chava! Blotted out for good! Then I got together some fresh dairy products and set off for Boiberik to my customers.

In Boiberik my customers welcomed me most enthusiastically: "How are you, Reb Tevye, why haven't we seen you such a long time?"

"How should I be," I answered. " *'We renew our days as of old'*—I'm the same *shlimazl* I always was, one of my cows has dropped dead."

"Why is it," they asked, "that all these miracles happen to you?" Then all of them and each one separately wanted to know what kind of cow I had lost, how much it cost me, and how many other cows I had left. Laughing merrily, they joked and made fun of me, a poor man, a *shlimazl,* as is the custom of rich people when they have just had a good meal, are in a cheerful mood, everything is fine and green outdoors, the weather is balmy—just right for a nice snooze. But Tevye is a person who can take a joke: not for the life of me would I have let them know what my feelings really were!

Having sold all my goods, I set off for home with my empty crocks and jars. Driving through the woods, I slackened the reins and let the horse go on slowly, so that he might stealthily crop a tuft of grass now and then. Losing myself in meditations, I let my imagination run away with me, thinking of life and of death, of this world and of the next, of what the world actually was, why a man lived, and similar things—all in order not to let myself think of Chava. But as if in spite, namely she, Chava, crept into my mind. Here she comes towards me, tall stately, beautiful and fresh as a pine tree, or as she was in early childhood, a tiny, sickly, almost lifeless little baby nestling in my arms, her head dropping over my shoulder. "What do you want, Chaveleh? Bread soaked in milk? A sip of milk?.."

For a while I forgot what she had done and my heart went out to her, my soul ached with longing for her. Then I remembered, and anger flared up in my breast against her, against him, against the whole world and against myself for not being able to blot out her memory, tear her out of my soul. Why can't I do it? Doesn't she deserve it? Was it for this Tevye had to be a Jew among Jews? Did he toil and suffer, root the ground, and raise children only for them to be torn away by force, to fall away as a pine cone falls from its tree, and to be carried away by the wind and by smoke? For instance, I thought, a tree, say, an oak, grows in the forest; then someone comes along with an axe and chops off a branch, another branch and another branch—what is the tree without its branches, alas? Better go, lummox, and chop down the whole tree and put an end to it! Why should an oak stand bare in the forest!..

As these thoughts flitted through my mind, my horse suddenly came to a standstill. What was the matter? I looked up and saw—Chava! The same Chava as before, hadn't changed a bit, not even her clothes were different!

My first impulse was to spring to the ground and embrace her, kiss her... But I was held back by a second thought: Tevye, what are you, a woman? I gave the reins a tug and cried to the horse: "Giddy-up, *shlimazl!*"—and pulled to the right. But Chava also went to the right, waving her hand to me, as if to say: "Stand still a while, I have to tell you something."

Something seemed to snap in me, something tugged at my heart, my limbs went weak and I all but jumped off the wagon! But I held myself in check and pulled the reins, making the horse turn left—Chava also moved left, looking at me wildly, her face deathly pale... What shall I do? I thought to myself. Shall I stop or drive ahead? Before I could look around she was already holding the horse by the bridle and crying: *"Tateh!* I'll sooner die than let you move from this spot! I beg you, please hear me out first, *Tateh*-Father!.."

Eh, thought I, you mean to take me by force? Oh, no, my dear! If that is what you mean—it's a sign that you don't know your father... And I began to lay into the poor beast for all it was worth. The horse lunged ahead obediently, turning its head backwards and twitching its ears.

"Giddap," I told the horse, *"'Judge not the vessel but its contents'*—don't look, my clever one, where you shouldn't." But do you think that I myself didn't want to turn my head and look back, to have at least a glimpse of the spot where she remained

"But Chava also went to the right, waving her hand to me."

standing? But no, Tevye is not a woman, Tevye knows how to deal with smoldering Satan...

Well, I don't want to waste your time with too long a story. If it was ordained that I should suffer the torments of the damned after death, I must surely have atoned for all my sins already. I know the taste of Gehenna and of purgatory, and of all the other tortures that are described in our Holy Books—ask me and I'll tell you!

All the rest of the way home it seemed to me that she was running after the wagon and crying: "Hear me out, *Tateh*-Father!" A thought crossed my mind: Tevye, you are taking too much upon yourself! What harm will it do if you stop for a while and hear what she has to say? Maybe she has something to say that you should know? Maybe, who knows, she has changed her mind and wants to cone back? Maybe she suffers in her life with him and wants you to help her escape from a living hell?.. Maybe, maybe and maybe and many another maybe flitted through my mind; again I saw her as a child and was reminded of the passage: *"As a father has mercy on his children..."*—a father can have no bad children, and I blamed myself and said that I *"do not deserve to be pitied,"* that I am unworthy of walking upon the earth!

So what? Why all this fretting and fuming, you stubborn madman? Turn your wagon back, you brute, and make it up with her, she is your own child, not another's! Strange thoughts crept into my head: What is the meaning of Jew and non-Jew?.. And why did God create Jews and non-Jews?.. And since He did create Jews and non-Jews, why should they be so isolated from each other, hate each other, just as if this one is from God and that one is not from God?.. I was sorry that I was not as learned as others in holy and in secular books, where I might have found the true justification for this...

In order to break up this train of thought I began to chant: *"Blessed are they who dwell in Thy house, and they shall continue to praise Thee...",* saying *Minhah,* the afternoon prayer, as God bade us.

But what good was this praying, this chanting, when inside, in my heart, an entirely different melody was playing: "Cha-va! cha-va! Cha-va!" The louder I chanted *"Blessed..."* the louder became the "Chava" tune, and the more I tried to forget her, the clearer was her image in my eyes, and it seemed to me that I could hear her voice crying: "Hear me out, *Tateh*-Father!" I tried to stop my

97

ears so as not to hear her, I shut my eyes not to see her; I chanted the *Shmin-esra* and could not hear my own voice, I beat my breast and called myself a sinner and did not know what my sin was; my life was in a muddle and I myself was bewildered. I told nobody of this encounter and spoke with nobody of Chava, asked nobody about her, although I knew very well where she was and where he was and what they were doing, but nobody would find out anything from me. My enemies won't live to see the day I complain to anyone. That's the kind of person Tevye is!

I should like to know whether all men are like this, or whether I alone am so crazy?

You know, for example, it sometimes happens... You won't laugh at me? I am afraid you will...

For instance, it sometimes happens that I put on my Sabbath coat and set off for the railway station; I am ready to get on the train and go out there, to them, I know where they live. I go to the ticket-window and ask the man to give me a ticket. He asks, "Where to?" "To Yehupetz..." So he says, "I know of no such city." So I say, "Then it is not my fault..." And I turn and go back home, take off my Sabbath coat and get down to work, to my dairy wares and the horse and wagon. As it is written: *"Each man to his labor"*—the tailor to his shears, the cobbler to his last.

Yes, you are laughing at me! What did I tell you? I even know what you are thinking. You are thinking: This Tevye, he is something of an imbecile!

Therefore, *"Up to here and no further"*—it's enough for today, I mean... Be well and strong, and write me letters. And, for God's sake, don't forget what I asked you: keep silent concerning this, don't make a book out of it. But if you do happen to write, write about someone else, not me. Forget about me. As the passage goes: *"And he was forgotten"*—no more Tevye the Dairyman!

1906

"I knew very well where she was and what they were doing."

Shprintze

I owe you a most hearty greeting, Mr. Sholom Aleichem, peace be with you and your children! Oh my, my—a good many years have gone by since we last met, how much water has flown under the bridge since then! The anguish both we and our people have had to put up with during these years! Kishinev, a "cosnetution," pogroms, troubles, evils*—oh, dear God, Almighty Lord of the World! But I am surprised—don't take it amiss—you haven't changed a hair, knock on wood, knock on wood! Now take a look at me: *"Behold, I look like a man of seventy,"* while I am not yet sixty. Do you see how white my hair has grown? Ah, it's *"the pain of bringing up children"*—what you have to endure from children! Is there anyone who has suffered so much pain from his children as I have? A new misfortune befell me—what happened to my daughter Shprintze is more terrible than all my other troubles. However, as you see, life goes on, for it is written: *"Perforce you must live."* Go on living, even though your heart is breaking as you sing this little song:

> *Of what use is my life, what's the world to me,*
> *When I have no luck and no money do I see?*

In short, as it stands written in Perek: *"The Holy One, blessed be He, wanted to grant merit..."*—God wanted to do his Jews a favor, so we were blessed with a new trouble, a cosnetution"! Oh, what a "cosnetution"! All of a sudden a tumult, a commotion broke loose among our rich ones, a stampede began from Yehupetz to foreign health resorts, allegedly on account of their nerves, to take warm baths and salt-water cures—all of it last year's snow and other non-

---

*Kishinev, "cosnetution", pogroms, troubles, evils. In 1903 a Jewish pogrom was instigated by the tsarist government in Kishinev, followed by numerous other pogroms; in 1905 the government was forced to cede a Constitution under pressure of the growing revolutionary movement in the land, but it did little to improve the life of the toiling masses.—*Tr.*

sense! When Yehupetz was deserted, Boiberik with its air and its woods and its *dachas* went to pot! As we say in the morning prayer: *"Blessed be He who bestows mercy..."* So what happened? We have a great God who rules the world and watches out for his poor wretches and makes sure that they suffer a little more on earth.

What a summer we had, oh my! Boiberik began to fill up with people running away from Odessa, from Rostov, from Yekaterinoslav, from Mogilev and from Kishinev—thousands of rich people, money-bags, millionaires! In their towns the "cosnetution" was, apparently, fiercer than with us in Yehupetz, because they kept coming and coming. One might have asked: Why do they come running to us? The answer is: Why do our people run to them? It has already become, thank God, a custom among us that no sooner do rumors of pogroms begin to spread than Jews start running from one town to another; as the Holy Book says, *"They journeyed and they encamped, they encamped and they journeyed"*—which means: you come to me and I'll go to you...

Meanwhile, as you may well imagine, Boiberik became a big town overflowing with people, with women and children. Now, children like to peck at foods, so dairy produce was in high demand. From whom, if not from Tevye, were dairy foods to be bought? So Tevye became the fashion. From all sides you heard nothing but Tevye and Tevye. Reb Tevye, come here! Reb Tevye, come to me! When God wills—why question it?

"And it came to pass..." It all began one day before *Shabuoth*. I bought some dairy goods to one of my customers, a rich young widow who had come to us from Yekaterinoslav with her sonny-boy, Aronchik, for the summer. You understand, of course, that her first acquaintanceship in Boiberik was with me.

"I've been told," she said, the widow, I mean, "that yours are the best dairy products."

"How could it be otherwise?" said I. "It is not for nothing that King Solomon says that a good name lets itself be heard, like the sound of a *shofar,* throughout the world, and if you like I can tell you what the *Midrash* has to say about that."

So she interrupted me, the widow, I mean, and told me that she was a widow and was unversed in such things. She didn't even know what it was eaten with. The main thing was that the butter should be fresh and the cheese tasty... Well, go talk to a female!..

In short, I began to come along to the Yekaterinoslav widow twice a week; every Monday and Thursday, punctually as a timetable, I would bring my dairy foods, without asking whether they needed them or not. I became an intimate in the household, as I usually do, and began to take a closer interest in the domestic affairs: stuck my nose into the kitchen, and told them a few times what I found necessary to tell them about running the house. The first time, naturally, I got a scolding from the servant-girl—she told me not to butt in, not to peep into stranger's pots. Next time my words were heeded, and by the third time they already asked my advice, because she, the widow, I mean, had by then realized who Tevye was.

It went on in this way until the widow disclosed her trouble, her affliction, her misfortune—Aronchik! He, a young man of twenty-and-something years, said his mother, cared for nothing but horses, bicycles and fishing, and beyond that—nothing! He wouldn't even hear of business, of making money. His father had left him, she said, a handsome fortune, almost a million rubles, but he took no notice of it at all. He only knew how to spend, he was foolishly open-handed!

"Where is he," I asked, "this boy of yours? You just turn him over to me, I'll have a little talk with him, edify him, quote a few proverbs, tell him a *midrash.*"

So she laughed: "A *midrash?* You'd better bring him a horse, not a *midrash!*"

Suddenly, as we were talking, *the lad arrived*—in came the young man, Aronchik, a lad stately as a pine tree, strong and good-looking, the picture of health. He wore a wide belt right over his trousers, begging your pardon, a watch was stuffed into a pocket in the belt, and his sleeves were rolled up above his elbows.

"Where have you been?" asked his mother.

"Out in a boat, fishing," he answered.

"A fine occupation," I said, "for such a lad as you. Back at home everything may be going to wrack and ruin while you catch fish here!"

I took a look at my widow—she was red as a beet. She must surely have thought that her son would grab me by the collar, deal me a couple of slaps and then throw me out like a piece of broken crockery. Nonsense! Tevye is not afraid of such things! I, when I have something on my mind, I go ahead and say it!

"And so it was." The young man, upon hearing such words, stepped back a little, crossed his hands behind his back, looked me over from head to toe, emitted a queer whistle, and suddenly burst

out into such laughter that both his mother and I feared he had lost his mind for a minute!

What shall I say? From that time on we became friends, real good friends! I must tell you that the longer I knew the lad, the more I liked him, even though he was a scamp and a spendthrift, far too free with his money, and something of a dolt, too. For instance, he could meet a poor man, thrust his hand into his pocket, pull out some money and hand it over to this man without counting it. Who ever heard of such a thing? Or he could take a good new coat off his own back and give it away. Talk about folly! I was really sorry for the mother! She used to complain to me, asked me what she should do, beg me to try and hammer some sense into his head. I, of course, did not begrudge her this favor— why should I? Did it cost me any money? So I began to sit down with him and tell him stories, give him examples, quote passages from the Torah and roll off *midrashim,* as Tevye knows how to do. He really became interested and seemed to enjoy listening to me. He kept asking me all sorts of questions: how did I live, what kind of a home did I have?

"I should like," he once said, "to pay you a visit some day, Tevye!"

"If anybody wants to visit Tevye," I answered, "he just picks himself up and drives over to Tevye's farmstead—you have enough horses and bicycles. And in a pinch it's no big deal to come over on foot—it's not far, you only have to cut through the woods."

"When," he asked, "are you at home?"

"I can be found at home," I answered, "only on the Sabbath, or on a holiday. Wait! You know what? Next Friday, God willing, is *Shabuoth.* If you want to stroll over to our farm, my wife will treat you to *blintzes* such as—and I added in Hebrew—*'our blessed ancestors never ate in Egypt!'*"

"And what does that mean?" he asked. "You know that I'm not at all strong in Hebrew quotations."

"I know," said I, "that you are weak. If you had gone to *heder,* as I did, you would know even *what the rebbitzen said*—what the rabbi's wife said."

So he laughed and said: "Done. You shall have me as a guest. I'll come to you, Reb Tevye, on the first day of *Shabuoth* with a couple of friends to eat *blintzes,* but you see to it that they are hot!"

"At *white heat, inside and out*—from the frying pan right into your mouth!" said I.

When I got home I called out to my old woman: "Golda, we'll have guests for *Shabuoth!*"

She immediately came up with: "*Mazl-tov,* congratulations, who are they?"

"That you'll find out later," said I; "you get a batch of eggs ready—we have plenty of cheese and butter, thank God. I want you to make enough *blintzes* for three guests, people that approve of eating and don't even begin to know anything of Rashi's commentaries."

"Oh, you must have picked up some *shlimazls* from the hungry lands?" said she.

"You're a fool, Golda," said I. "First of all, it wouldn't be such a calamity if we should, God forbid, feed a poor man with *Shabuoth blintzes.* Secondly, be informed, my dear spouse, my modest and pious wife Madam Golda, that one of our *Shabuoth* guests will be the widow's boy, the one who is called Aronchik—I told you about him."

"Oh," she said, "that's a different story."

The power of millions! Even my Golda, when she gets a whiff of money, becomes an altogether different person. That's the way of the world, what do you think? How does it go in *hallel? "Gold and silver, the work of man's hands"*—money is the undoing of man...

Well, the bright, green Holy Day of *Shabuoth* came. How beautiful, how green, how bright and warm it is out in the country when *Shabuoth* arrives I don't have to tell you. Your richest man could only wish to have such a blue sky, with such a green forest, with such fragrant pines, such lush green, pasture land for the cows that stand chewing their cud and looking at you as if to say: "Give us such grass all the time and we won't begrudge you any milk!"

No, you may say whatever you like, tempt me with the best livelihood to move from the country to the city—I won't exchange places with you. Where have you such a sky in the city? As we say in a *hallel: "The Heavens are the Heavens of the Lord"*—it's God's own sky! when you look skyward in town what do you see? A brick wall, a roof, a chimney—but where will you find such trees? And if some wretched tree does manage to survive, you cover it over with a cloak!..

104

However that may be, my guests were full of admiration when they came to my farm on *Shabuoth*. They came, four young men, on horseback, their horses—one better than the other! As for the prancer Aronchik was seated on, it was a real gelding, the likes of which you wouldn't be able to buy even for three hundred rubles!

"Welcome, guests," I greeted them. "Is it in honor of *Shabuoth* that you've come on horseback?* No matter, Tevye is not too pious, and if, with God's help, you should be whipped in the next world the pain won't be mine... Hey, Golda," I called, "see to the *blintzes,* and let the table be carried out here into the fresh air. There is nothing inside the house I could boast of to our guests... Hey, there, Shprintze! Taibl! Beilke! Where are you? Get a move on you!"

My orders were obeyed: the table was carried outside, chairs were placed around it, a tablecloth laid, plates, spoons, forks, salt brought out, and very soon Golda appeared with the *blintzes,* piping hot, right from the frying pan, plump and tasty! My visitors couldn't praise them enough...

"What are you standing there for," I said to Golda, "go and repeat the same verse over again. Today is *Shabuoth,*" I said, "so the same prayer has to be said twice!"

Golda immediately filled up another platter and Shprintze served the *blintzes* at the table. Suddenly I saw, as I glanced at Aronchik, that he couldn't take his eyes off my Shprintze! What had drawn his attention to her? "Eat," I said to him, "why aren't you eating?"

"What else am I doing if not eating?" said he.

"You are looking at Shprintze," said I.

At this everybody began to laugh, my Shprintze too. Everybody felt so happy, so good—a good, joyous *Shabuoth*... Go and foresee that from this merrymaking would spring a misfortune, a lament, an evil, God's punishment on my head, the blackest misery and suffering on my soul!

But man is a fool. A sensible man mustn't let anything get to his heart, he must understand that things are as they should be, for if they should have been otherwise, they wouldn't have been as they are! Don't we say in the Psalms: *"Put thy trust in God."* Put your faith in God and He will already see to it that you are doubled up

---

*Jewish religious laws forbid riding on anything or in any conveyance on the Sabbath and on holidays.—*Tr.*

under your load of misery and still keep on saying: *"This too, is for the best."* Listen to what can come about in this world, but listen carefully, because this is where the real story actually begins.

"It was evening and it was day." Late one afternoon I came home, dead-tired after my day's work, exhausted by the running from *dacha* to *dacha* in Boiberik. Hitched to my front door I saw a familiar horse. I was ready to swear that it was Aronchik's prancer, the one I had then judged to be worth three hundred rubles. I went up to the horse, slapped his rump, tickled his neck and ruffled his mane. "Well, well, my beauty," I said to the horse, "What are you doing here?" The animal turned his winsome face to me and looked at me with his clever eyes, as if to say: "Why ask me? Ask my master."

I went inside and began to question my wife. "Tell me, Golda my love, what is Aronchik doing here?"

"How should I know," she answered, "he is one of your buddies, isn't he?"

"So where is he?"

"He went with the children for a stroll in the woods," she answered.

"Why suddenly a stroll?" said I and asked her to give me supper. When I had eaten I began to think: what is it, Tevye, that upsets you so? When a person comes to visit you, do you have to get so rattled? Quite the opposite...

As I was thinking this I looked outside and saw my girls walking with the young man, holding bouquets of freshly-picked flowers, the two younger ones, Taibl and Beilke in the lead, followed by Shprintze and Aronchik.

"Good evening!"

"The same to you."

Aronchik stood there with a strange look on his face, patting his horse and chewing a blade of grass. Then he turned to me:

"Reb Tevye! I want to do business with you—let's exchange our horses."

"You haven't found anyone else to play jokes on?" I asked.

"No," said he, "I'm in earnest."

"So you're in earnest," said I. "How much, for instance, does your horse cost?"

"How much would you value it at?" he asked.

"I value it," said I, "at three hundred rubles, and perhaps even a bit over that."

He laughed and said that the horse cost more than three times that sum, and then asked: "Well? Is it a deal?"

This talk was not at all to my liking: What did he mean by offering to exchange his expensive horse for my outspent *shlimazl* of a hack? So I told him to put off business for another time and jokingly asked him whether that was really the reason for his visit. If that was so, I said, it was a waste of his travel expenses...

To this he answered me quite seriously: "Actually, I came for another reason. If you like, let us take a little walk."

Why this urge for walking? I thought to myself as I accompanied him to the nearby grove.

The sun had gone down some time ago, it was already darkish in the green grove, the frogs were croaking at the dike, and the fragrance of the grass was balm to the soul!

Aronchik walked and I walked along with him. He was silent and so was I. Then he stopped, cleared his throat, and said:

"Reb Tevye! What would you say, for instance, if I told you that I love your daughter Shprintze and want to marry her?"

"What I would say? I would say that one madman's name should be erased and yours put in its stead," I answered.

So he looked at me and exclaimed: "What do you mean?"

"Just what I said!"

"I don't understand you."

"That's a sign," said I, "that you are not so very bright. As it is written: *'A wise man hath his eyes in his head,'* which means that a smart man understands a wink, while a fool needs a stick."

This rather offended him. "I speak to you plainly and you answer me with witticisms and quotations!" he said.

To this I said: "Every cantor sings as he can, and every preacher preaches for himself. If you want to learn what kind of preacher you are, talk this thing over with your mother first, she will make everything quite clear to you."

"Apparently," said he, "you take me for a child that has to ask his mother what to do?"

"Of course you have to ask your mother," said I, "and she will certainly tell you that you are an imbecile, and she will be right."

"She will be right?" he asked.

"Of course she will be right," said I. "What kind of a husband are you for my Shprintze? Is she your equal? And, what is most important, what kind of a relative-by-marriage am I for your mother?"

"If that's the case, Reb Tevye," said he, "you are greatly mistaken! I am no eighteen-year-old youngster, I seek no in-laws to please my mother. I know who you are and who your daughter is. She suits me, and that's the way I want it to be and that's how it will be!"

"I beg your pardon for interrupting you," said I. "I see that you've already finished with one side. Have you already made sure of the other side?"

"I don't know what you mean."

"I mean my daughter, Shprintze. Have you already spoken to her about this, and what does she say?" I asked him.

This seemed to offend him, but he laughed and answered: "What a question! Of course I have spoken to her, and not just once but several times—I come here every day."

You hear that? He'd been coming here every day and I knew nothing! You're a cow, Tevye, in human likeness! You should be given straw to chew! If you permit yourself to be led by the nose you'll be bought and sold before you know it, you donkey!

Thinking thus, I walked back to the house with Aronchik; he said goodbye to my gang, mounted his horse and *"departed like Moses"*—trotted away to Boiberik.

And now let us, as you say in your books, leave the prince and turn to the princess, to Shprintze....

"Listen, daughter," said I, "there is something I want to know: you tell me how come that Aronchik talked to you about such a matter without my knowing anything about it?" Do you get any answer from a tree? I got the same answer from her! She lowered her eyes and blushed like a bride, but didn't as much as utter a word!

Bah, I thought to myself, you don't want to talk now, but you'll talk a little later…Tevye is not a woman, he can wait!

I waited for some time, for, as it is said, *"his day will come"*; then at a moment when the two of us were alone, I said: "Shprintze, answer my question: do you at least know him, this here Aronchik?"

"Of course I know him," was her answer.

"Do you know that he is a whistler?"

"What do you mean—a whistler?"

"An empty nutshell that whistles when you blow into it."

To this she said: "You are mistaken, Arnold is a fine person."

"*I want you to tell me, but quite openly, how much this will cost us, all told.*"

"He is already Arnold to you," said I, "not Aronchik the char-latan?"

"Arnold," said she, "is no charlatan, Arnold has a kind heart. Arnold lives in a house of mean-minded people who know nothing but money and money."

"Oho," said I, "so you, too, Shprintze, have become an enlightened philosopher. You also despise money?"

In short, from this talk I understood that things had gone pretty far with them, and that it was a little too late to undo them, for I know my children. Tevye's daughters, as I already told you once, when they fall in love, it's with heart and soul and body! And I thought: Fool! Why should you want, Tevye, to be wiser than the whole world? Maybe it is God's will that through this shy little Shprintze you should be succored, be rewarded for all the blows and pains you have endured; maybe it was ordained that you should live well in your old age and learn how good life can be in the world? Perhaps it was fated that you should have a million-airess for a daughter? And why not? It doesn't suit you? Where is it written that Tevye must be a poor man forever, that he must always drag himself around with his nag, delivering cheese and butter to the rich Yehupetz gluttons!? Who knows, perhaps it was destined from above that in my old age I should redress the wrongs of the world, become a benefactor, a hospitable host, and maybe even sit down with Jewish scholars and study the Torah?

These and other shining, golden thoughts entered my mind. As it is said in the morning prayer, *"Many thoughts are in man's heart,"* or, as the peasants, begging your pardon, say: *Duren dumkoyo bogateyet*—a fool gets rich only in his thoughts.

I came into the house, took my old woman aside and started a conversation with her: "What, for instance," I asked, "would happen if our Shprintze became a millionairess?"

So she asked: "What is a millionairess?"

"A millionairess means the wife of a millionaire."

"And what is a millionaire?"

So I explained: "A millionaire is a man who has a million."

"How much is it, a million?" she asked.

To this I said: "If you're such a simpleton and don't know how much a million is, then what is there to talk to you about?

"Who asks you to talk?" was her retort. And that was also true.

Well, a day went by and I came home in the evening. "Has Aronchik been here?" I asked. "No, he hasn't...."

110

Another day went by: "Was the lad here?" "No, he wasn't."

To go to the widow on some pretext was unbecoming; I didn't want her to think that Tevye was eager for the match. Actually I felt that for her all this was like *"a rose among thorns,"* like a fifth wheel to a wagon. Although I couldn't understand why. Just because I didn't have a million? But now I had a relative-by-marriage who was a millionairess! But whom was she getting for a relative? A poor Jew, a pauper, a Tevye the Dairyman. So who had more reason to be proud, she or I? I'll tell you the plain truth: I began to want this match, and not so much because of the match itself as for the satisfaction of getting the better of them.

Damn them all, the rich Yehupetzers, let them know who Tevye is! Up to now one heard nothing but Brodsky and Brodsky, as if all the rest weren't human beings at all!

Thus I reflected, driving home from Boiberik. When I came into the house my wife welcomed me with good news: "A messenger was here just now from Boiberik, from the widow. She wants you to come there at once, without fail; even if it is the middle of the night, you must hitch up the horse and go to her; they want to see you very badly!"

"What's got into them?" I asked. "What's the great hurry, why haven't they got any time?" I looked at Shprintze—she was silent, only her eyes spoke, and how they spoke! Nobody could understand what was in her heart as I could....

I had been afraid all the time—anything was possible—that the whole affair might come to nothing, so I said everything I could think of against him, that he was this and he was that; however, I saw that it was like being up against a blank wall, and my Shprintze was wasting away like a candle.

I hitched up the horse again and set off towards evening for Boiberik. As I went along I thought to myself: Why should they summon me in such haste? To say something? About the betrothal? He could have come to me for that, I think. I am, after all, the girl's father. But this notion made me laugh: Who in the world has heard of a rich man coming to a poor man?! It could only happen when the end of the world came, in the time of the Messiah. The time that will soon come, as those young whelps wanted to convince me, when the rich and the poor will be equal, share and share alike, mine is yours, yours is mine and other such nonsense! It seems to me that ours is a clever world, and yet such fools live in it! Well, well, well!

With these thoughts I reached Boiberik and drove directly to the widow's *dacha*. I stopped the horse—where was the widow? No widow! Where was the young man? No young man! Then who sent for me?

"I sent for you!" said a roly-poly little man with a plucked beard and a thick golden chain across his pot-belly.

"And who are you?" I asked.

"I am the widow's brother," said he, Aronchik's uncle... I was summoned by a telegram from Yekaterinoslav and have just arrived"

"If that is so, then *sholom aleichem* to you," said I and sat down. When I had seated myself he said: "Sit down."

"Thanks," said I, "I am already sitting. So how do you do, and how does the 'cosnetution' do in your part of the world?"

To this he gave me no answer, plumped himself down in a rocking-chair, his hands in his pockets, his pot-belly with the golden chain bulging out, and addressed me with the following words:

"You are called, I think, Tevye, aren't you?"

"Yes," said I, "when I am called up to read the Torah they say: 'Arise, Reb Tevye, son of Shneyer-Zalman.' "

"Listen to me, Reb Tevye," said he, "of what use are long discussions? Let us go right to the issue, to the business at hand."

"With pleasure," said I. "King Solomon said a long time ago: *'For everything there is a time'*—when business has to be spoken of, let it be business. I am," said I, "a businessman."

"It's evident that you are a man of business. That is why I want to talk to you as one merchant to another. I want you to tell me, but quite openly, how much this will cost us, all told?.. But speak quite frankly!"

"If," said I, "we are to speak openly, frankly, then I must own up that I don't know what you are talking about."

"Reb Tevye!" said he, without taking his hands out of his pockets. "I am asking you how much, all told, this business will cost us?"

"That depends," said I, "on the kind of wedding you have in mind. If you decide upon a swell wedding, as is fitting for you, I'm not in a position to foot it."

He stared at me in surprise and said: "Either you are playing the fool, or you really are a fool... Although you don't look like a fool, because if you were one you wouldn't have managed to lure my nephew into this morass. You invited him to your home allegedly for *Shabuoth blintzes,* showed him a pretty girl who may or may not be your daughter—I don't care to go into such details—and he fell in love with her, that is, he liked her. Well, and that she, too, liked him, that of course goes without saying, we are not questioning that. I don't know, perhaps she is an honest child and is in earnest, I won't go so far into the matter... But you mustn't forget," he went on, "who *you* are and who *we* are. After all, you are a sensible person, how could you even presume that Tevye the Dairyman who brings us cheese and butter might become related to us by marriage?.. So what if they gave each other their word? They can take their word back! There is no great misfortune in that, and if his breach of promise has to cost us something we have nothing against paying. A girl is not a boy, whether she is your daughter or not, I don't care to go into such details."

God Almighty! What does the man want? thought I.

Meanwhile, he doesn't stop talking over my head for a moment; I needn't think, says he, that I could contrive a scandal, spread it about that his nephew, says he, had proposed to Tevye the Dairyman's daughter... And I should knock out of my head the notion that his sister was the kind of person from whom money might be pumped... If there was no trouble she wouldn't mind paying a few rubles: she would put it down to charity... We are human beings, after all, sometimes you have to help a person...

You want to know how I answered him? I said nothing, woe is me. *"My tongue clave to the roof of my mouth"*—I lost the power of speech! I got up, turned my face to the door—and fled, as if escaping from a fire, from prison!

There was a buzzing in my head, a shimmering before my eyes, and the man's words seemed to repeat themselves in my ears: "Speak openly..." "A daughter or not a daughter..." "A widow to be pumped..." "Put it down to charity... "

I went to my horse, covered up my face and—you won't laugh at me?—I burst into tears. I wept and wept! When I had had a good cry I got into the wagon and laid into my horse, and only then did I ask God a question, as Job once asked: "What hast Thou seen in old Job, dear Lord, that Thou never leavest him be for a moment? Are there already no other people in the world?"

When I got home I found my gang, knock on wood, in a merry mood. They were eating supper, only Shprintze was missing. "Where is Shprintze?" I asked.

"What happened," they asked, "why were you sent for?"

113

"I sprang from my wagon... but when I got there it was already all over..."

So I repeated my question: "Where is Shprintze?"

And they again asked: "What happened?"

"Nothing, why should anything happen? Thank God, all is quiet, nothing is heard about any pogroms."

At these words Shprintze came in. She took one look into my eyes and sat down at the table, just as if the whole thing had nothing to do with her... Her face showed nothing, only this quietness of hers was a bit too much, unnatural.

I didn't like this sitting of hers, lost in thought, and her blind obedience. Told to sit—she sits, told to eat—she eats, told to go—she goes, and when her name is called she jumps. When I looked at her, my heart ached and an anger burned in me—I didn't know against whom. Oh, dear God in Heaven, Almighty Lord, why do you punish me so, for whose sins?!!

Well, shall I tell you the end of the story? Such an end I wouldn't wish on my worst enemy, and it would be wrong to wish it on anyone, for the misfortune of children is the worst curse in the chapter of *Admonitions!* How do I know, maybe someone did put that curse on me? You don't believe in such things? So what else can it be? All right, let me hear what you think. But what is the good of such a discussion. Listen to the end of my story.

One evening I was returning from Boiberik with a heavy heart. Just imagine the sorrow and the shame, and how I pitied my child! And what about the widow, you may ask? And her son? What widow? What son? They left without even saying goodbye! It's a shame to admit it—but they didn't even settle their debt to me for cheese and butter... But that is not what I'm talking about; they probably forgot. I'm speaking of the way they left without even saying goodbye!.. What the poor child went through, no other human being except me knew, for I am a father, and a father's heart understands...

Do you think she said even a single word to me? That she complained? Or wept even once? Eh! Then you don't know Tevye's daughters. Quiet, withdrawn, she kept her grief to herself, but she flickered and melted away like a candle! Once in a while she would sigh, but that sigh was enough to tear my heart asunder!

So I was driving along homeward, deep in sad thoughts, asking our Heavenly Father questions and answering them myself. It wasn't God who was bothering me so much—with Him I had already made it up, one way or another. People, that's who worried me; why should people make life bitter both for others and for themselves, when they could live well and happily? Could it be that God created Man so that he should suffer on earth? Of what use was that to Him?...

With such thoughts I drove into my farmstead. From afar I saw a crowd of people by the dike—men, women, lads, girls and small children without count. What could it be? It was not a fire. Maybe somebody had drowned—went bathing by the dike and found his death? Nobody knows where the angel of Death awaits him, as we say in the hymn describing the Day of Judgment.

Suddenly I saw my Golda running, her shawl flying, her hands stretched out before her, and in front of her my daughters Beilke and Taibl, all three of them screaming, wailing: "Daughter! Sister! Shprintze!!!"

I sprang from the wagon—I don't know how I didn't break my neck—and ran to the river, but when I got there it was already all over....

What did I want to ask you? Oh, yes! Have you ever seen a drowned person? Never ?..

When a person dies he usually dies with his eyes closed...The eyes of one who has drowned are open—do you know the reason for this?...

Please excuse me, I've taken up too much of your time, and I myself am also not a free man; I have to go to my horse and deliver my wares. The world is a world. One must think about earning a living, too—and forget what has been. Because it is said that one must forget what the earth has covered, and while a man lives he cannot part from his soul. Witticisms are of no help, and we must return to the old adage saying that as long *"as my soul abides within me"*—plod on, Tevye!

Goodbye, be well, and if you think of me sometimes, don't think ill of me.

1907

Tevye Goes to Palestine

As told by Tevye the Dairyman while traveling in a train

Look who's here! How are you, Reb Sholom Aleichem? What fine company! I never even dreamed of it! My best greetings, and peace be with you! I wondered all the time and thought and thought: What's happened, why is it that he is seen neither in Boiberik nor in Yehupetz such a long time? Anything could've happened: maybe he has settled all his accounts and left us altogether—moved to the place where black radishes and chicken fat are not eaten? On the other hand, I thought, can it be possible that *he* should do such foolishness? He is, after all, a sensible person, as I live! Well, thank the Lord for seeing you in good health, as it is written: *"A mountain with a mountain..."*—a man with a man....

You are looking at me, Panie*, as if you can't recognize me. I am your good old friend, Tevye. *"Look not at the vessel but at its contents"*—don't let my new coat deceive you. This is the same *shlimazl* Tevye as before, to a hair, but when you get dressed up in your Sabbath clothes you begin to look as if you were somebody, maybe even a rich man. When you go out among people you can't do otherwise, especially if you are going on such a long journey, to Palestine, no small matter.

You look at me and think: How come such a simple little person as Tevye, who dealt all his life in dairy foods, should suddenly get such an idea into his head, a thing only someone like Brodsky could allow himself in his old age? Believe me, Mr. Sholom Aleichem, *"it is altogether puzzling"*—this expression is all around true. Please move your valise a little and I'll sit down here opposite you and tell you my story—just listen to what the Almighty can do....

Panie—Sir, Mr. (Polish) — *Tr.*

"I am your good old friend Tevye...don't let my new coat deceive you."

But before I begin I must tell you that I have for some time now been a widower, may this never happen to you. My Golda, God rest her soul, is dead. A simple woman, without learning, with no pretensions, but she was very devout and pious. Let her intercede in the other world for her children; they made her suffer enough in this one and perhaps were even the cause of her leaving before her time. She couldn't bear their having scattered in different directions—one this way, the other that way. "Alas," she would say, "what is left of my life, neither child nor chick! Even a cow," she said, "longs for its calf when it is weaned away from her..."

That's how she spoke to me, my Golda, shedding bitter tears. I watched the woman waning from day to day like a candle; my heart went out in pity for her, and I said to her: "Eh, Golda darling, in our *Rosh Hashono* prayer it says: *'Im k'vonim im k'vodim'*— whether we're like children or like slaves. With children or without children—it's all the same! We have a great God, a kind and strong God, but still," said I, "I should have as many blessings as the times the Almighty plays one of His tricks, my enemies should have such luck."

But she, may she forgive me, was, after all, only a woman, and so she said to me: "You are sinning, Tevye, you mustn't sin."

"Oh, come on," said I, "did I say something bad? Did I say anything, God forbid, against the ways of the Almighty? For since He has created His world so wonderfully, so that children are not children and parents are no better than dirt," said I, "then He, of course, knows what He is doing."

But she didn't understand me, her mind was wandering: "I am dying, Tevye," she said; "who will cook supper for you?"

Her voice was barely audible and she looked at me with such eyes that even a stone would be touched. Tevye, however, is not a woman, so I answered her with a saying, with a quotation from the Bible, with a *midrash* and another *midrash:*

"Golda," I said, "you've been a faithful wife to me for so many years, so you won't make a fool of me in my old age."

As I said this I took a look at my Golda—it was the end!

"What's the matter, Golda?"

"Nothing," she barely whispered.

I saw that the game was in favor of the devil, so I hitched up my horse and drove to town and brought back a doctor, the best doctor. When I got home—oh my, oh me! My Golda was already stretched out on the floor with a candle burning at her head; she looked like a little mound of earth raked together and covered with a black cloth.

I stood and thought: *"That is all that man is!"*—so this is the end of a human being!? Oh, Almighty God, the things you've done to your Tevye! What will I do now in my old age, a wretched and miserable man? And with that I fell to the ground.

But go weep and wail! What's the use? Listen to what I want to tell you. When you witness death closely you become a heretic and begin to think: *"What are we and what is our life?"* And what is this entire world, with the wheels that turn, the trains that rush along crazily, with its entire tumult and bustle all around, and even Brodsky with his millions—vanity of vanities, altogether nonsense and trash.

Well, I hired a man to read *kaddish* for her, for my wife Golda, may she rest in peace, and paid him for a whole year ahead. What else could I do, if God had punished me, given me no males, only females, only daughters and daughters, no good man should ken them! I don't know if everybody has such trouble with their daughters, or if, perhaps, only I am such a miserable *shlimazl* who has no luck at all with them? That is, I have nothing against my daughters themselves, and luck is as God wills. I should have at least half of what my girls wish me. Quite the opposite, they are too devoted to me, and everything that is "too" is in excess. Take, for instance, my youngest, her name is Beilke. What idea can you have of the kind of child she is? You have known me, thank God, for a year and a day, and you are aware that I am not the kind of father who sits down and begins to praise his children just for the sake of talking. But since I've mentioned my Beilke, I must say just this: Since God began to deal in Beilkes he never created *such* a Beilke! Her beauty we won't even discuss. Tevye's daughters, you know that yourself, are famous far and wide as great beauties. But she, Beilke, puts all the others into the shade! A beauty of beauties! But that is not all. In regard to my Beilke, one may truly quote the words from *A Woman of Valor: "Charms are deceitful"*—I am speaking not of looks but of character. Gold, pure gold, I tell you! From the first I was always the cream of the crop with her, but since my Golda, may she rest in peace, passed away, I became the apple of Beilke's eye! She wouldn't let a speck of dust fall on me. I already said to myself: the Almighty, as we say in our prayer, *"precedes anger with mercy"*—God sends remedies for a scourge. However, it's hard to tell which is worse, the remedy or the scourge!

Go be a prophet and guess that Beilke would, on my account, sell herself for money and send her father in his old age to Palestine! That's only in a manner of speaking, of course. She is just as much to blame for this as you are. The whole fault is his, her chosen one's. I don't want to curse him, may a barracks collapse over him! Then, perhaps, if we should want to think the matter over carefully, to dig a little deeper, it might turn out that I am more guilty than anyone else, for there is a passage in the *Gemara* that says: *"Man is obligated..."* but it's a fine thing, as I live, that I should have to tell you what the *Gemara* says!

Well, to make it short—I don't want to keep you too long. One year went by, then another, my Beilke grew up, became, knock on wood, of a marriageable age, while Tevye went on with his trade, driving, as always, his horse and wagon, and delivering cheese and butter to Boiberik in the summer, to Yehupetz in the winter—may a deluge flood it, as it once did Sodom. I can't stand that city, and not so much the city itself as the people, and not all the people, but one man—Ephraim the Matchmaker, may the devil take him and his father's father! Now listen to what a matchmaker can do to you.

"And there came the day..." I come to Yehupetz once in the middle of September with my wares. I give a look— *"Haman approacheth"*—Ephraim the Matchmaker is coming towards me! I once told you about him. Although Ephraim is a pesky person, but no sooner do you see him than you must stop—that's the kind of power this man has.

"Ho, there, my sage," I say to my horse, "stand still a while, I'll let you have something to chew." I stop Ephraim the Matchmaker, greet him, and begin to talk to him in a roundabout way:

"How is business?"

He answers, with a deep sigh: "Bad."

"How come?"

"Nothing to do," says he.

"Nothing at all?"

"Nothing at all!"

"What's the matter?" I ask.

So he says: "The trouble is, that matches are no longer concluded at home."

"Where then are matches concluded now?" I ask.

"Somewhere out there, abroad," says he.

"So what, for instance, should a man like me do, whose grandfather's granny never set foot there?"

"For you, Reb Tevye," says he, offering me his snuff-box, "I have a piece of goods right here on the spot!"

"Namely?" I ask.

"A widow without children, has a dowry of a hundred and fifty rubles, used to be a cook in the very best houses," says he.

I give him a nasty look. "Reb Ephraim, for whom do you propose this match?"

"For whom should I propose it if not for you!" says he.

"Of all the wild and crazy notions—may they fall on my enemies' heads!" I shout and give my horse a taste of the whip, meaning to drive away, but Ephraim stops me:

"Please excuse me, Reb Tevye, perhaps I have offended you. But tell me, who did *you* have in mind?" he asks.

"Who should I have in mind," says I, "if not my youngest daughter?"

At this he suddenly springs back and slaps his forehead: "Wait! It's a good thing you reminded me, a long life to you, Reb Tevye!"

"Amen, the same to you, may you also live until the coming of the Messiah. But what's the matter with you," I ask. "Why the great rejoicing?"

"It's good, it's unusually wonderful, Reb Tevye, it couldn't be better in the entire world!" he cries.

"What, namely, is this goodness, tell me?"

He answers: "I have a match worthy of your youngest daughter, a piece of luck, a grand prize, a rich man, very rich, a millionaire, a Brodsky. He is a contractor and his name is Padhatzur."

"Padhatzur? A familiar name from the Bible," said I.

"What Bible," says he, "where Bible? He's a contractor, this Padhatzur, he builds houses, brick buildings, bridges. He was in Japan during the war and brought back heaps of gold. He drives around in carriages drawn by fiery steeds, he has footmen at his door, there is a bathroom right in his own house and furniture from Paris, and he wears a diamond ring on his finger. He is not at all old, not married, a real bachelor, top quality! What he is looking for is a pretty girl; it doesn't matter who she is, she may be naked and barefoot, as long as she is a beauty!.."

"Whoa, there!" say I to him. "If you fly so fast, without stopping to graze your horse, we'll find ourselves, Reb Ephraim, at the other end of nowhere. Besides, if I am not mistaken, you once tried to fix up this very same match for my older daughter, for Hodel."

Upon hearing these words of mine, he, Ephraim, began to laugh so hard that he had to hold his sides. I thought the fellow would have a stroke!

"Oh," he exclaimed, "you're thinking of the time my grandmother was brought to bed with her first child! That fellow went bankrupt before the war and ran away to America!"

"May the memory of a righteous person be blessed," said I. "Maybe this one will run there, too?"

This outraged the matchmaker terribly:

"What are you talking about, Reb Tevye? That one was," said he, "a good-for-nothing, a charlatan, a spendthrift, while this one is a contractor since the war, with a business, with an office, with clerks, with... with... with..."

What can I say—the matchmaker got so excited that he pulled me off my wagon, grabbed me by the lapels and began to shake me, and he wouldn't let go until a policeman came up and wanted to take both of us to the police station. A lucky thing it was that I remembered the Biblical passage which says: *"You may take interest from a stranger"*—you've got to know how to handle the police...

In short, why take up so much of your time? This Padhatzur became my youngest one's, my Beilke's, betrothed. And *"the days were not long"*—I mean, it did take quite some time before we raised the wedding canopy. Why do I say that it took some time? Because she, Beilke, was as eager for this match as one is eager for death. The more this Padhatzur showered her with gifts, with gold watches and diamond rings, the more loathsome did he become to her. Things don't have to be spelled out to me, you know. I understood this very well from the look in her eyes and on her face, and from the tears she shed in secret. I thought it over and once remarked, as if in passing:

"Listen, Beilke," I said, "I'm afraid that your Padhatzur is just as much to your liking as to mine, as sweet to you as he is to me, isn't he?"

She turned fire-red and asked:

"Who told you that?"

"Why then do you cry all night?' I asked.

"Do I cry?"

"No," said I, "you don't cry, you sob. You think that if you bury your head in a pillow you'll hide your tears from me? You think that I, your father, am a little boy, or that my brain has dried up and I don't understand that you are doing this for your old father? That you want him to be provided for in his old age, so that he should have a place to lay his head, and wouldn't have to, God forbid, go begging from house to house? If that is what you think," said I, "then you are a big fool. We have a great God and Tevye is not one of those ten loafers who sits down to the bread of charity. Money is worthless, as it says in the Bible. Take, for instance, your sister Hodel, a pauper, one might say, and yet," said I, "look what she writes, from the devil knows where, from the ends of the earth, and how happy she says she is with her *shlimazl* Feferl!"

Now, you try and guess what she, Beilke, replied!

"Don't compare me with Hodel," she said. "Hodel's time was a time when the whole world rocked on its foundations, it was on the verge of turning upside-down; people were concerned about the world and they forgot about themselves. Nowadays, the world is a world again, so that each one is concerned with himself and the world is forgotten..."

That is how Beilke answered me—try and understand what she meant!

Well, you are something of an expert on Tevye's daughters aren't you? But you should have seen her during the marriage cere-mony! A princess! Gazing at her in delight, I thought to myself: Is this Beilke, Tevye's daughter? Where did she learn to stand so, to walk so, to hold her head so, and to dress so that her clothes looked as if they had been poured out over her body?

However, I wasn't allowed to admire her for long; on the very day of the wedding, about half-past five in the afternoon, the new-lyweds got up and left; they departed by an express train for the devil knows where, for "Nataliye"*, as is fashionable among rich people. They returned when winter had already come, around *Hanukkah,* sent me a message saying that I was to come to them in Yehupetz *immediately* and *without fail.* This made me think: If they had just wanted to see me, they would simply have asked me to come, that's all. But why the *immediately* and *without fail?* Probably something important was up—but what? All sorts of thoughts, both good and bad, flitted through my mind: Maybe the couple had already quarreled out there, and were on the verge of divorce? But at once I reproached myself: You're a fool, Tevye, why do you always expect bad things? How do you know why they

---

*Italy (distorted).—*Tr.*

have sent for you? Maybe they miss you and want to see you? Or perhaps Beilke wants her father to be near her? Or it may even be that Padhatzur wants to give you a job, take you into his business and make you a supervisor over his contracts?... Anyhow, I had to go. So I got into my wagon and *"went forth to Heron."* To Yehupetz.

Along the way, I let my imagination run free. I saw myself abandoning the village, selling the cows, the horse and wagon, all my goods and chattels, and moving into town. There I would become first a supervisor in Padhutzur's business, then his cashier, and then the manager of all his building contracts, and after that a partner in all his business affairs, fifty-fifty, and I would drive around just as he did, behind a pair of fiery steeds, one a bay, the other a chestnut. And I began to think in amazement about myself: *"What is this and what is it all for?"* How come such a modest little man, Tevye, to deal with such important affairs? What do I need all this hullabaloo for, this never-ending day-and-night fair with its bustle and tumult? How does it go— *"to seat them with the mighty"*—to hobnob with millionaires? Let me be, I want a quiet and peaceful old age, I want to be able to look into a volume of the *Mishnah* from time to time, to read a chapter from the Book of Psalms—one has to have the next world in mind sometimes, too, isn't that so? As King Solomon said: Man is verily like the cattle, he forgets that no matter how long he lives he will have to die some day...

With these thoughts and visions I arrived in Yehupetz and drove directly to Padhatzur's house. To boast to you of his *"grandeur and wealth"*—that is, of his home and its furnishings— of that I am not capable. I've never had the honor of visiting Brodsky in his home, but I am certain that there can be nothing finer than my son-in-law's house! You will understand what sort of mansion it was if I tell you that the man who guarded the door, a lanky fellow with silver buttons, would by no means let me in, do what you will. So how was I to get in? Through the glass door I could see him, may his memory be forgotten, brushing clothes. I winked at him, spoke to him in sign language, showing him by gestures that he should let me in, for the master's wife was my own daughter... But he understood nothing, the lout, and motioned to me, also in sign language, to go to blazes, to go my way, that is. Such a pig-headed idol! Just think, to visit your own daughter you've got to have pull?

Woe unto your gray head, Tevye, look what you've lived to! Such was my thought as I looked through the glass door. Then I noticed a girl moving about inside. Must be one of their housemaids, I decided, marking her shifty eyes. All housemaids have shifty eyes. I am a frequent visitor in many wealthy houses and I know all the maids in them. So I winked at her: "Open up, kitty!" She obeyed, and opened the door and asked me, in Yiddish, "Who do you want?'

"Does Padhatzur live here?" I asked.

"Who do you want?" said she in a louder voice.

But I said, still louder: "When you are asked a question you should answer. *First things first*—does Padhatzur live here?"

"He does," she answered.

"If that is the case we speak the same language. Go and tell your Madam Padhatzur that she has a guest, her father Tevye has arrived, and he's been standing outside for quite a while like a beggar at the door, because he didn't have the honor," I said, "to find favor in the eyes of that Esau with the silver buttons who isn't worth your littlest fingernail!"

Having heard me out, the maid giggled impudently, slammed the door in my face, ran upstairs, then downstairs again, opened the door for me and led me into a real palace, such as my grandfathers' grandfathers never saw even in their dreams. Silk and velvet, gold and crystal, and when you walked you didn't even hear your own footsteps, for your sinful feet were treading on the most costly rugs, soft as snow. And clocks! Clocks on the walls, clocks on the tables, clocks without end! Good Lord! Have you many more of this kind in the world? What does a person need so many clocks for? Such were my thoughts as I walked, my hands clasped behind my back, a little further on. Suddenly I saw several Tevyes at once on all sides, one Tevye going here, another going there, one coming towards me, another walking away from me. Confound it! Mirrors on all four sides! Only such a bird as this contractor could afford so many clocks and so many mirrors!

Here Padhatzur came to my mind, a fat, roly-poly little man with a bald head who speaks in a high voice and doesn't laugh but snickers. I recalled how he came to me in the village for the first time with his fiery steeds; he made himself at home at once—as if he were in his father's vineyard! Got acquainted with my Beilke, then called me aside and whispered a secret into my ear—but so loudly you could have heard it on the other side of Yehupetz.

126

What was this secret? The secret was that my daughter had found favor in his eyes and he wanted "one-two-three and a wedding canopy." That my daughter had found favor in his eyes was not difficult to understand, but this "one-two-three" was *like a double-edged sword*" to me—as if a blunt knife had pierced my heart. What did he mean by "one-two-three and a wedding canopy"? And what about me? And what about Beilke? Oh, didn't I just long to give him a couple of quotations from the Bible and a *midrash* to remember me by! But on the other hand, I thought, why should you, Tevye, interfere? Did it help you a lot with your elder daughters, when you tried to advise them against their choices? You rattled like a drum, poured out your whole Torah, and who was the fool at the end? Tevye!

Oh, well, as the story-books say, let us leave the prince and turn to the princess.

Well, so I obliged them and came to Yehupetz. They greeted me affectionately: *"Sholom aleichem!" "Aleichem sholom!"* "How are you?" "How are things with you?" "Be seated!" "Thank you, I'm quite comfortable." And all the other ceremonies, as is the custom.

It didn't seem proper to ask them first why, *"Today of all days,"* they had sent for me. But Tevye is not a woman, he can wait.

Meanwhile, a tall man-servant in enormous white gloves came in and said that lunch was already on the table, so all three of us got up and went into a room entirely made up of oak: an oaken table, oaken chairs, oaken wainscotting, an oaken ceiling, everything elaborately carved and painted and designed. On the table was a royal spread: tea and coffee and chocolate, shortbread and pastries, fine cognac, the best appetizers, salted and pickled dainties, and all manner of other delicious foods, fruits, and vegetables. I'm ashamed to say this, but I'm afraid that at her father's table my Beilke never saw such delicacies.

Well, they poured me a drink, then another. Drinking to their health and looking at her, at Beilke, I thought: At last you have lived to see the day, Tevye's daughter, as we say in *Hallel:* "*Who raiseth up the poor out of the dust*"—when God helps a poor man— "*and lifteth up the needy out of the dunghill,*" the man becomes altogether unrecognizable. She seems to be Beilke, and yet not Beilke.

I remembered the other Beilke, from the past, and I compared the two Beilkes—and my heart ached. It was just as if I had struck a bad bargain, had done something that couldn't be undone. Let us say, for instance, I felt as if I had exchanged my hard-working

"Suddenly I saw several Tevyes at once, on all sides."

little dobbin for a colt without being able to tell what would become of it in the future—a horse or a block of wood.

Eh, Beilke, Beilke, thought I, what has become of you? Remember how you used to sit at night by a smoky lamp, sewing and humming to yourself, or how you would go out and milk two cows in a flash, or roll up your sleeves and cook me a simple borsht, or a dish of dough pellets with beans, or cheese-filled dumplings, or bake me some poppy-seed cookies, and you would say: "*Tateh,* go wash your hands!" This was, for me, the best of all melodies!

Now she sat there with her Padhatzur like a queen; two footmen were waiting at the table, clattering the plates—and she, Beilke? She didn't say a single word! He, Padhatzur, talked for both of them, his mouth didn't shut for a moment! Never in my life have I seen anyone who was so fond of jabbering, of chattering the devil knows what, without stopping his snickery laughter. Of such types it is said: he makes his own jokes and laughs at them himself.

Besides the three of us there was a fourth person at the table, a red-cheeked character. What and who he was I don't know, but that he was no mean eater was self-evident. All the time Padhatzur talked this guest went on gorging himself; as it says in Perek: "*Three who have eaten*"—he certainly ate enough for three.

This one ate and that one talked, and all of it such empty things, I couldn't care a hoot about: podryad*, gubernskoye pravleniye**, udelnaya vedomost***, kaznacheistvo†, Japan...

Of all this the only thing that held some interest for me was Japan, because I had had something to do with that country. During the war, as you know, horses were in great demand and were sought for high and low. Of course, the authorities got to me, too, and they took my horse to task, measured him with a yardstick, drove him back and forth and then gave him a white card††. Well, I told them that I'd known beforehand that their trouble was in vain, for, as the Bible says: "*The righteous man knoweth the soul of his animal.*" Tevye's horse is not a horse that goes to war.

But please excuse me, Mr. Sholom Aleichem, I get one thing confused with another and am apt, God forbid, to stray from the

---

*Contract (Russian).—*Tr.*
**Provincial Board of Directors (Russian).—*Tr.*
***Royal Family Real Estate Register (Russian).—*Tr.*
†The Exchequer (Russian).—*Tr.*
††A certificate giving exemption from military service.—*Tr.*

highway. As you say, let us get back to business—to my story.

Well, so we ate and drank our fill, as God bade us. When we got up from the table, he Padhatzur, took my arm and led me into a separate chamber—his "study"—a royally decorated room with rifles and spears on the walls, and tiny cannons on the table. He seated me on a sort of sofa, soft as butter, took out, from a golden box, two thick, aromatic cigars and lighted them, one for himself, one for me. Then he sat down opposite me and said:

"Do you know why I have sent for you?"

Aha, thought I, he probably means to have a talk with me about business. But I played dumb and said "'Am I my brother's keeper?'—how should I know?'

"I wanted to have a talk with you—about you yourself," said he.

Must be about a job, I thought to myself, and said: "If only it is something good—my pleasure, let's hear it."

He took the cigar out of his mouth and began a whole speech:

"You are," said he, "no fool and so you won't take offense if I speak to you frankly. You must know that I do business on a large scale, and when one engages in such big business deals..."

Yes, thought I, he has me in mind. And I interrupted him and said: "As the *Gemara* says in the Sabbath chapter: *'The more business, the more worries.'* Do you know," I asked him, "how this passage from the *Gemara* should be explained?"

He answered me quite frankly: "I'll tell you the honest truth: I never studied any *Gemara* and I don't even know what it looks like."

That's how Padhatzur answered me and burst into his snickery laughter.

How do you like that? I would think that if God has punished you by making you an ignoramus, then let it at least be covered up, why go boast about it? Thinking so, I said to him:

"I did figure that you hadn't much to do with such things, but let's hear what you have to say further."

So he went on: "Further, I wanted to tell you that with my business and my name, with my *polozheniye**, it doesn't suit me that you are known as Tevye the Dairyman. I want you to know that I am *lichno*** acquainted with the Governor, and it is quite

---

*Standing, social status (Russian).—*Tr.*
**Personally (Russian).—*Tr.*

130

possible that Brodsky might come to visit me, or Polyakov, or maybe even Rothschild, *chem chort nye shutit?***"

That's what he said to me, this Padhatzur, and I just sat there looking at his shiny bald head and thinking: It may very well be that you are personally acquainted with the Governor, and that Rothschild might come to your house some day, but you talk like a despicable cur... And I said, with a bit of resentment:

"So what can be done if Rothschild does indeed come to see you?"

You think he understood the dig? *There was neither bear nor woods*—he understood nothing!

"I wanted you," said he, "to give up this dairy business and occupy yourself with something else."

"Namely with what?"

"With whatever you like," he said, "there are lots of businesses in the world! I'll help you out with money, if only you stop being Tevye the Dairyman. Or, hold on," said he, "why not pick yourself up one-two-three and go to America? Eh?"

After saying this he pushed his cigar back into his mouth and looked me straight in the eye, his bald head glistening...

Well? How does one answer such a crude fellow? My first thought was: Why are you sitting, Tevye, like a clay *golem?* Get up, kiss the *mezuzah,* slam the door and get out without as much as a goodbye! It really made my gall rise! The impudence of this contractor! What does he mean, telling me to give up my own respectable business and go away to America? Just because Rothschild might visit him some day, Tevye the Dairyman must fly to the ends of the world?!

My heart was boiling with anger like a kettle, and I was already upset from before this talk. My wrath was directed against her, against my Beilke: Why are you sitting there like a queen amidst the hundred clocks and the thousand mirrors, while here your father, Tevye, is running the gauntlet over live coals? As I live, I thought, your sister Hodel made a better marriage than you! It is true, of course, that she doesn't have such a house with so many expensive gew-gaws as you have, but she has Feferl for a husband, and he is a fine human being, a man who doesn't think of himself—his concern is for the whole world... And, in addition, he has

---

*"What doesn't the devil joke about?" A Russian saying, which means, "you never can tell."—*Tr.*

131

a head on his shoulders, not a pot with a shiny lid on it! And what a tongue he has, this Feferl—gold and gold! He, when you give him a passage from the Bible, comes back at you with three! Just you wait, my dear contractor, I'll quote you a passage that'll make your head spin!

That is what I thought, and then addressed him with the following words:

"Well, it's no great matter that the *Gemara* is a closed book to you—this I forgive you. When a Jew sits in Yehupetz and his name is Padhatzur and he is a contractor," said I, "the *Gemara* may well be forgotten in the attic. But a simple passage even a peasant in bast shoes will understand. You know, of course, what the *Targum* says about Laban the Aramaean: '*Hafromtah lapigstailah hakanmaknoh lafurhatah.*'"

He stared at me and asked: "What, then, does it mean?"

"It means," said I, "that from a pig's tail no fur hat can be made."

"In regard to what do you say that?"

"In regard to your bidding me to go to America."

Emitting his snickery laughter, he said:

"If not to America, then perhaps to Palestine? All old Jews go to Palestine..."

No sooner had he uttered these words than they sank into my brain as an iron nail sinks into wood: Stop! Maybe this isn't at all so bad, Tevye, as you might think? Maybe it is a good plan? Because rather than have such pleasure from children as you have, Palestine is perhaps better? What do you risk and whom do you have here? Your Golda, may she rest in peace, is already in the grave, while you yourself, God forgive me, haven't you suffered enough? How much longer can you tread the earth?

Actually, Mr. Sholom Aleichem, I must confess that I have for a long time cherished a dream to visit Palestine: I would like to stand by the Wailing Wall, by the tombs of the Patriarchs and Mother Rachel's Tomb, and see with my own eyes the river Jordan, Mount Sinai and the Red Sea, the cities Pithom and Raamses, and other such things. My imagination carried me away to the blessed Land of Canaan, "*the land flowing with milk and honey,*" but he interrupted my reflections, this Padhatzur, right in the middle, saying:

"Well? What is there to think about so long? One-two-three..."

"With you, praise the Lord," said I, "everything is one-two-three... For me it's a difficult piece of the *Mishnah,* because to pick oneself up and travel to Palestine one has to have the wherewithal..." At this he emitted his snickery laughter, got up, went to his desk, took a purse from a drawer and counted me out a goodly sum of money. I immediately understood what he meant, took the wad—the power of money!—and put it deep down into a pocket. I wanted to quote a few passages and a *midrash* for his edification, to round everything up, but he paid no attention at all to my words and said:

"This will be more than enough to get you there, and when you arrive at your destination and need more money, write us a letter and it will be forwarded to you one-two-three... I hope you won't have to be reminded again about leaving, for, after all, you are a man of honor, a man with a *sovest.**"

That is how my son-in-law Padhatzur spoke to me with his snickery laughter that crept right into one's entrails.

I suddenly caught myself thinking: Why not fling the money right back into his face and quote a passage to the effect that Tevye is not to be bought for money, and with Tevye you don't speak of honor and of conscience?

However, before I could open my mouth to say something he rang a bell, called in Beilke and said to her:

"Dushenka**, you know what? Your father is forsaking us, he is selling everything he has and is going away one-two-three to Palestine."

"I dreamed a dream but I do not understand it"—I dreamed it the other night and last night! So I thought to myself and looked at my Beilke—not a trace of any emotion on her face. Stood there as if rooted to the floor, not a drop of blood in her face, looking from him to me, from me to him—and not a single word! I watched her and also said nothing, so the two of us were mute, as it is written in the Psalms: *"...my tongue clave"*—we had both lost the power of speech. I felt dizzy, a pulse was beating in my temples as if I had breathed charcoal fumes. What could be the reason? Perhaps, thought I, it's from that fine cigar that he gave me to smoke? Yes, but he is also smoking, this Padhatzur! Smoking and talking, his mouth doesn't shut at all, although his eyelids are drooping as if he's ready to fall asleep.

---

*Conscience (Russian)—*Tr.*
**Dearest, darling, sweetheart (Russian)—*Tr.*

"First you've got to go," said he, "from here to Odessa on the express train, and from Odessa by sea to Jaffa. Right now is the best time for traveling by sea, because later the winds and snows and storms begin and—and—and…" He mumbled, his words were getting jumbled as if he were falling asleep, but he didn't stop his chatter: "and when you are ready for the journey you'll let us know and we'll both come to the railway station to see you off, because who knows when we'll see each other again?"

These words were followed by a gaping yawn, begging your pardon; he got to his feet and said to her, to Beilke: "*Dushenka,* you sit here a while and I'll go and catch forty winks."

You've never said a better thing, as I live! At least now there is someone on whom I can pour out the bitterness of my heart! This is what I said to myself, intending to take my Beilke to task, to give her a good scolding for everything that had piled up in my heart that morning, but now she, Beilke, fell on my neck and began to weep. How do you think she wept? My daughters, may no evil befall them, are brave, they keep up their courage, but then, when it comes to something, they suddenly break down and the tears begin to flow from them as the sap flows from a tapped birch. Take, for instance, my older daughter Hodel. How she carried on, how she wept when she had to leave to share her Feferl's exile in the cold lands! But there is no comparison: that one can't even hold a candle to this one!

I'll tell you the honest truth: I myself, as you already know me, am not a man who is ready with his tears. I wept long and bitterly only once, when my Golda, may she rest in peace, was lying on the ground, and once more I wept when Hodel went off to join her Feferl and I was left standing by the station like a big fool, all alone with my little horse; then, maybe another couple of times it happened that I, as you say, blubbered a little, but I don't remember that I ever made a habit of weeping. Now Beilke and her tears wrung my soul so that I couldn't restrain myself and I didn't have the heart to say even one cross word to her. To me you don't have to explain things. My name is Tevye. I soon understood the reason for her tears. They weren't just tears; they were, please understand me, tears for *"the sin I have sinned before thee,"* for not having listened to her father… So instead of giving her a piece of my mind and pouring out all my wrath against her Padhatzur, I began to console her with such an example and such an example, as Tevye can. She listened to me, my Beilke, and then said:

134

"No, *Tateh,* that is not why I'm crying. I have no complaints against anyone, I am crying because you are going away on account of me and I can do nothing about it. This is what torments me so."

"There, there," said I. "You talk like a child, you've forgotten that we still have a great God and that your father still possesses all his senses. For your father," I continued, "it's no big deal to travel to Palestine and come back, as it is written: *'They journeyed and they encamped'—tuda i nazad—*there and back again."

I tried in this way to comfort her, but to myself I thought: Tevye, you're lying! When you leave for Palestine it'll be *"may he rest in peace"*—no more Tevye!..

Just as if she could read my thoughts, Beilke said to me:

"No, *Tateh,* that is how you comfort a little child. You give it a doll, some plaything to hold and tell it a pretty story about a little white kid... If it comes to storytelling," said she, "let *me* tell *you* one. But the story I want to tell you, *Tateh,* is more sad than beautiful."

That is how she spoke to me, my Beilke. Tevye's daughters don't speak in vain. She gave me a whole song and dance, told me a saga, a story from the *Arabian Nights,* how this Padhatzur of hers had lifted himself from the lowest depths to the highest levels, all by his own wits, and now he sought the glory of having Brodsky visit his house; to achieve this he was handing out donations, simply pouring out rubles by the thousand in all directions. However, money alone was not enough, you had to have "lineage," too, so he, Padhatzur, that is, was moving heaven and earth in order to show that he was not just anybody. He boasted that he was descended from the great Padhatzurs, that his father was also a famous contractor. "Although," said Beilke, "he is fully aware that I know that his father was a poor musician. Now he tells everybody that his wife's father was a millionaire..."

Whom does he mean?" I asked. "Me? Maybe I *was* once destined to have millions some day, but that will have to suffice me!"

"Oh, *Tateh,*" said Beilke, "if you only knew how I blush when he introduces me to his acquaintances and starts telling them what important people my father, my uncles and my whole family are— pure fantasy! But I have to endure all this, listen and keep mum, because he is very capricious in these matters."

"You call it 'caprice,' " said I, " but to me it sounds like abomination and downright chicanery."

135

"No, *Tateh,*" said Beilke, "you don't know him, he is not at all as bad as you think. Only he is a man whose moods change frequently—one minute he is like this, the next like that. He is really kindhearted and generous. A mournful mien on a person's face will prompt him, if the moment is propitious, to do anything for this person. As for me—why, nothing is too good for me! You think I have no influence at all with him? Not long ago I persuaded him to rescue Hodel and her husband from their distant exile. He swore to me," she said, "that he would spend thousands on it, but on one condition—that they go from there directly to Japan."

"Why to Japan," said I, "why not to India, or, for instance, to *Padan-Aram** to visit the Queen of Sheba?"

"Because he has business in Japan," she answered. "He has business dealings all over the world; what he spends in a day on telegrams alone, our whole family could have lived on for six months. Yes, but what good is all this to me when I am no longer myself!"

"It comes out," said I, "as we read in the *Perek: 'If I am not for myself who will be for me?'*—I am not I, you are not you."

So I spoke to her, here a saying, there a quotation from the Holy Book, although my heart bled to see how my child suffered *"in riches and in honor,"* as we say.

"Your sister Hodel," I said, "would have done differently." But she, Beilke, interrupted me:

"I've already told you, *Tateh,* that you shouldn't compare me to Hodel. Hodel lived in Hodel's time, and Beilke lives in Beilke's time... From Hodel's time to Beilke's time the distance is as great as from here to Japan."

Do you understand the meaning of such strange talk?

Oh, I see that you are in a hurry, Mr. Sholom Aleichem. Another two minutes and all my stories will end. Satiated with the worries and anguish of my lucky youngest daughter, I left the house *"in mourning and with bowed head"*—completely crushed and beaten. I flung away the cigar, the fumes of which had made my head spin, and shouted after it—after the cigar, that is:

"Go to limbo, damn you!"

"Whom do you mean, Reb Tevye?" asked a voice behind my back. I turned my head and took a look—it was he, Ephraim the Matchmaker, may the Evil One catch him!

---

*A place mentioned in the Bible. Here meant in an ironical sense—"to some other place". —*Tr.*

"Welcome, whom do I see!" I exclaimed. "What are you doing here?"

"What," said he, "are *you* doing here?"

"I am visiting my children."

"And how are they?" he asked.

"How," said I, "should they be? We should be as lucky!"

"As I see," said he, "you are quite pleased with my merchandise?"

"And how pleased!" said I. "May God repay you many times over."

Thanks for your kind words; perhaps you might add a gift to your blessings?" he said.

"Why, didn't you receive your matchmaker's fee?" I asked.

"He shouldn't have more himself, this Padhatzur of yours."

"What was wrong," I asked, "too small a sum?"

"Not so small a sum as the 'goodwill' that went with it!"

"What do you mean?"

"I mean," said he, "that it's all gone already—not a single *grosz* left!"

"Where did it go to?" I asked.

"I married off a daughter," he answered.

"Congratulations," said I, "may God grant them good luck and you should live to have joy from them."

"Great joy," he retorted, "I have already lived to have from them. I landed me a scoundrel of a son-in-law. He beat and tortured my daughter, picked up the few rubles, and went off to America."

"Why did you let him go so far?"

"What should I have done with him?"

"You should have sprinkled salt on his tail," said I.

"You are evidently in a cheerful mood, Reb Tevye?"

"God grant you at least half of it, oh, Lord Almighty!" said I.

"So that's how it is? And I thought you were a rich man! But since you aren't—here's a pinch of snuff for you!" said he.

Having gotten rid of the matchmaker with his pinch of snuff, I drove home and began to sell off my household goods, objects that had accumulated over the years. Mind you, such things aren't done as quickly as you speak of them. Every pot, every trifle cost me a piece of my health. This reminded me of Golda, may she rest in peace, that reminded me of the children, God Bless them. But nothing hurt me so much as parting from my horse. Looking at him I felt guilty. So many years we had toiled together, suffered together, gone hungry together, and suddenly I take and sell him! I sold the horse to a water-carrier, because from teamsters you get nothing but insults. I went to them to sell my horse, so they said:

"God be with you, Reb Tevye, do you call this a horse?"

"What then is it—a candlestick?"

"No," they said, "it's not a candlestick you have here, it's a *Lamed-Vovnik*—one of the Thirty-Six Saintly Ones."

"What is that supposed to mean?"

"It means," they said, "an ancient creature of thirty-six years without a vestige of teeth, with a gray lip and trembling sides— like an old woman on a frosty Sabbath eve!"

How do you like such teamster-talk? The poor horse, I could swear, understood every single word, as it is said in the Holy Book: *"The ox recognizes a buyer"*—an animal knows when it is being put up for sale. You want proof? When I closed the deal with the water-carrier and said "good luck to you," my little horse suddenly turned his winsome face to me, and the look in his patient eyes seemed to say: *" 'So this is my lot for all my labors?'*—this is how you thank me for my service?.." I looked for the last time at my horse as the water-carrier led him away to teach him a harsh lesson, and I remained standing there all alone, thinking: Almighty God! How wisely You manage Your little world! You have created a Tevye and created his horse, and the same good luck befalls both of them! A human being, however, has a mouth and can at least complain, unburden his heart, but what can a horse do? Alas, it is but a dumb beast and, as it is said, herein lies *"the advantage of man over beast."*

You are looking, Mr. Sholom Aleichem, at the tears in my eyes, and you probably think: This Tevye apparently grieves for his horse? Why, dear man, for my horse? I grieve for everything, and I will miss everybody. I will miss the horse, I will miss the village, I will miss the village elder and the village policeman, I will miss the Boiberik summer people, the rich Yehupetzers, and even Ephraim the Matchmaker, a plague on him, because when all is said and done, what is he but a poor wretch trying to make a living?

When, God willing, I get safely to the place I am going to, I don't know what I will do there; but it's as clear as day that first of all I will go to Mother Rachel's Tomb. I will pray there for my children, whom I will probably never see again, and I will also keep Ephraim the Matchmaker in mind, him and you and all the Jews. Now let us shake hands, be well, a happy journey to you, and give my regards to each and every one.

1909

The "Fiddler on the Roof"—an American imagination.

Get Thee Out

My heartiest greetings to you, Mr. Sholom Aleichem! *Peace be with you and your children!* I've long been looking out for you, I have a whole pile of "merchandise" collected especially for you. I've asked: *"Where are you?"*—why don't I see you anymore? I was told that you have been traveling all over the world, in faraway lands, as it is said in the *Megilah,* the Book of Esther: *"The one hundred and twenty-seven provinces of Ahasheurus..."*

But it seems to me that you are looking somewhat strangely at me? Apparently, you are thinking: Is it he or not he? It is he, Mr. Sholom Aleichem, it is he! Your old friend Tevye, Tevye the Dairyman in person, the same Tevye, but no longer a dairyman, just an ordinary Jew, an old man, as you see, although in years I am not so old. As it is said in the *Haggadah: "Here I am, a man of seventy..."* but it's still quite a way off to seventy! Oh, why is my hair so white? Not from joy, believe me, dear friend. Partly my own troubles are to blame, not to complain, and partly the troubles of our people—a bad time! A bitter time for Jews...

However, I know what's pinching you—it's something else. You've probably recalled that we once said goodbye to each other when I was about to leave for Palestine. You must therefore be thinking that you see Tevye after his return from Palestine, and you probably already want to hear about my visit to Mother Rachel's Tomb and the Cave of Machpelah and other such things? Rest assured, if you have the time and want to hear a remarkable story, then listen attentively, as it is written: *"Hear ye!"* You will see for yourself that man is a mute beast and that we have a mighty God who rules over the world.

What portion of the Torah is being read in the synagogue this week? *Vayikro*—"Leviticus"? But I've been introduced to an altogether different chapter—*Lech-lecho*—"Get thee out!" "Get thee out, Tevye," I was told, *"begone out of thy country"*—out of your village where you were born and lived all your life, *"to the land which I will show thee"*—wherever your eyes lead you... And when was Tevye given this lesson to learn? When he had already become old and weak and forlorn; as we say in our prayers on *Rosh Hashono:* *"Do not cast us off in our old age!"*

But I'm running ahead of my story, I clear forgot that we were speaking of how things were in Palestine. How should things be going on there, my friend? It is a fine country—both of us should be as lucky— *"a land flowing with milk and honey,"* as it is said in the Torah. But the trouble is that Palestine is in Palestine, while I, as you see, am still here, *"outside of the Promised Land."* In the *Megilah,* Esther says: "If I perish I perish." These words, I tell you, must have been written about Tevye. A *shlimazl* I was and a *shlimazl* I'll die. There I stood, one foot almost on the other side, in the Holy Land, it only remained to buy a ticket and board a ship— and away! So what does God do? He thinks up something else for me. Just you listen.

My elder son-in-law, Motl Kamzoil, the Anatovka tailor, Heaven preserve us, lies down hale and hearty and goes and dies! That is, he never actually was what one might call robust. How could it be otherwise? He was, alas, only a poor workman, day and night he sat either *"absorbed in study or in worship of God"*—plying his thread and needle, patching, I beg your pardon, pants. So he sat and worked until he got the chest disease, and once it began, he hawked and coughed until he coughed up the last bit of his lungs. Nothing helped him, neither doctor nor medicine, goat's milk nor chocolate with honey. He was a fine person; it's true he was no scholar, but he was an honest man with no pretensions, and how he loved my daughter—simply adored her! He sacrificed himself for the children, and would have given his life for me!

So, *"Moses passed away."* Motl died and left me holding a bomb: how could I ever think of Palestine then? I already had a fine Holy Land right in my home! How, I ask you, could I leave a widowed daughter and her little orphaned children without a piece of bread? On the other hand, one might think, how could I help her when I myself was a sack full of holes? I couldn't bring her husband back to life, return their father from the other world to her children, and, besides, I myself am also nothing more than a sinful man: in my old age I wanted to rest my bones, to feel myself a human being, not a beast of burden. Enough fuss and bother! Enough of seeking the pleasures of this world! Some thought must be given to the next world, too, it's already high time! All the more so, since I had already played havoc with my bit of chattels: the horse, as you know, I had let go some time before, sold off my cows, and had only a pair of bull calves left that might perhaps become something worthwhile in the future if properly tended and foddered... And now suddenly go and become, in my old age, a provider for orphans, a father to small children!

But do you think this is all? Wait a while! The most important part is still to come, for if one trouble strikes at Tevye you may be sure that another one is following fast on its heels. For instance, once a misfortune befell me—one of my cows fell, so right after that—such a thing shouldn't happen to you—a second one lay down and died....

That is how God created His world, and so it will remain—nothing can be done about it!

Well, you remember the story of my youngest daughter Beilke, the grand prize she won, the big fish she caught—that Padhatzur, the bigshot, the contractor who made a fortune in the war and brought sackfuls of money to Yehupetz and fell in love with my daughter—he wanted a beautiful wife; he sent Ephraim the Matchmaker to me, may his name be forgotten... implored on his knees that she marry him, almost had a stroke, took her as she stood, without any dowry, and bedecked her from head to toe with gifts, diamonds, jewels... Great luck, wasn't it? Yes, well, all this luck flowed away like a river, and what a river! A river and a bog, God save us! When God orders the wheel of fortune to turn back, everything starts falling buttered side down; first, as we say in a *hallel*, it is *"who raiseth up the poor out of the dust,"* but before you know it—bang—and it becomes *"That looketh down low upon Heaven and upon the Earth"*—into the pit together with the traces!...

God loves to play with a human being. Oh, how He loves it! How many times did He play in this manner with Tevye: up and down! The same thing happened to my contractor, to Padhatzur. You probably remember how proud he was of his house in Yehupetz, with his thirteen servants, with his mirrors, clocks, and gew-gaws? Faugh, fah, fie! I think I told you, if you remember, how I tried to get my Beilke to make him buy this house in her name? They paid as much attention to my words as Haman does to a rattle—what does a father understand? He understands nothing! So what do you think the outcome was? My enemies should have such an outcome: in addition to going bankrupt, losing everything, having to sell all the mirrors and clocks and his wife's jewelry, he also got mixed up in some messy business, and had to flee the country and go to where the holy Sabbath goes—to America, that is. All heavy hearts go there, so they went, too. At first they had a very hard time in America. The little cash they had was soon used up, and when there was nothing to chew, the poor things had to go to work; they worked at all kinds of backbreaking jobs, toiled as the Jews toiled in Egypt, both he and she! She writes that now things are easier, thank God: they operate a stocking machine and are "making a living"... That's what they call it out there, in America, but here we would say "living from hand to mouth." It's a lucky thing, she writes, that there are only two of them, with neither chick nor child. *"That too is for the best."*

So now I ask you, doesn't he deserve to be cursed with the foulest curses—I mean Ephraim the Matchmaker? For the wonderful match he arranged for me, for the dirty mess he got me into! Would she have been worse off if she had married, say, a workman, as Tzeitl did, or a teacher, as Hodel did? Oh, they didn't have it too good, either? One is a young widow, the other is in exile with her husband at the back of nowhere? But that's as God wills it—what can man foresee?..

You know, she was really a wise woman, my Golda, may she rest in peace: she took a look around in good time, said goodbye to this foolish world and departed to the next one. Don't you think that rather than endure *"the pain of bringing up children"* I have suffered on account of my daughters, it is a thousand times better to lie peacefully in the grave?.. However, our *Perek* says: *"Perforce you must live"*—a man cannot take his fate into his own hands, and if he does he gets rapped over the knuckles...

Meanwhile we've strayed from the road and therefore *let us return to our original subject*—let us leave, as you say in your storybooks, the prince and return to the princess. Where were we? At lesson *Lech-lecho*—"Get thee out!" But before we begin *Lech-lecho* I want to ask you to be so kind as to stop with me for a while at *Balak*—the lesson of Vengeance. It has been the custom, since the world began, to first study *Lech-lecho* and later *Balak,* but with me it was the other way round: I was taught *Balak* first and then *Lech-lecho.* You might as well hear how *Balak* was taught to me; it might come in handy some day.

It happened some time ago, soon after the war, at the height of

"We've come, Tevel, to beat you up."

the "cosnetution," when *"salvations and consolations"* for the Jews—the pogroms—began, at first in the big cities, later in the small towns. But they never reached me, nor could they have done so. Why? Very simple! When you live for such a long time among Gentiles, down-to-earth Esaus, you are on friendly terms with all the householders of the village. *"Friend of the soul and Father of mercy"*—*"Batiushka* Tevel"* was held in high esteem! Advice is needed—"whatever Tevel says," a medicine against a fever—"go to Tevel," a loan without interest—again Tevel. Then why should I think about such things, about pogroms? Nonsense! The peasants themselves had told me many times over that I had nothing to fear, they wouldn't let anything happen to me! But *sure enough—* I'll tell you a fine story, just listen!

One day I came home from Boiberik—I was still hale and hearty then, in full feather, as they say—I still dealt in cheese and butter and various greens, too; I unharnessed my horse, threw it some hay and oats, and all of a sudden—I hadn't even had time to wash my hands before eating—my yard was full of peasants. The whole community had turned out, from the *starosta*—the village elder—Ivan Poperilo, down to the cowherd Trokhim, and they all, to my mind, had a strangely festive look…At first my heart even missed a beat—what sort of a holiday was this all of a sudden? Could they have come to teach me a harsh lesson? But on the other hand, I immediately had a second thought: Feh, Tevye, you should be ashamed of yourself! All your life you've lived here, one Jew among so many Gentiles, in peace and in friendship, and nobody ever did you the slightest harm!…

So I went out into the yard and greeted the crowd warmly: "Welcome, my dear friends, what brings you here? What's the good word? What news have you for me?..!

The *starosta,* Ivan Poperilo, stepped forward and said, quite openly and without any preliminaries at all:

"We've come, Tevel, to beat you up."

How do you like that? "Beating about the bush" is what we call it, language of implications, that is.…

You can imagine how I felt. But to show them my feelings— oh, no, quite the opposite! Tevye is not a little boy…

"*Mazl-tov!* Congratulations, children!" I exclaimed quite cheer-

---

*"Father," also "my dear fellow"—an obsolete respectful form of address; also "Father" in addressing a priest (Russian).—*Tr.*

fully. "But why so late? In other places they've already almost forgotten about such things!.."

Ivan Poperilo, the *starosta,* that is, now said, very earnestly:

"You've got to understand us, Tevel. We're been hesitating, trying to decide whether we should give you a beating or not. All around, in other places, your people are being scourged, so why should we leave you out? So we, the whole village, have decided that we must punish you... But we don't know exactly what to do to you, Tevel: either only knock out all the window-panes and rip up the feather-beds and pillows, or burn down your house and barn, and all your goods and chattels?"

These words really brought a chill to my heart. I looked at these neighbors of mine as they stood there leaning on their long staffs, whispering to each other. It looked as if they really meant business. If so, I thought to myself, as it says in the Book of Psalms: *"The waters are come in even into the soul"*—you are in real trouble, Tevye! Something must be done, but what? *"Do not give Satan an opening."* Eh, Tevye, I said to myself, with the Angel of Death one plays no games, I must think of something to tell them!

Well, my dear friend, I won't go into all the details, but a miracle was apparently ordained and the Almighty kept up my courage; I said to them, to the peasants, good-naturedly:

"Please listen to me, gentlemen! Hear me out, my dear neighbors: since the whole community has decided so, it means that you probably know best that Tevye deserves to have his entire property and chattels ruined by you... Only you must know," said I, "that there is a Higher Power than your village community! Are you aware that there is a God in the world? I do not mean *my* God or *your* God, I am speaking of the God who is everybody's God, who sits up there in Heaven and sees all the meanness and vileness that goes on down here... It may be," I went on, "that He Himself has marked me down to be punished for nothing, innocently, through you, my best friends, but it may also be that, on the contrary, He by no means wants any evil to befall Tevye... Who can know what God wants? Perhaps one of you will undertake to find out?.."

In short, they apparently understood that they wouldn't get far with Tevye; the *starosta,* Ivan Poperilo, addressed me as follows: "It's like this, Tevel. Actually, we have nothing against you. You are a Jew, of course, but not a bad man. However, that is neither here nor there—we must do something to you. The community passed

146

such a decision—we can't go back on it! At least," he said, "we'll smash your windows. This we must do, for it somebody drives through our village, let them see that we've punished you, otherwise we'll be fined..."

Such were his exact words, just as I told them to you, so help me God in all my undertakings! Now I ask you, Mr. Sholom Aleichem, you are, after all, a man who has traveled all over the world—isn't Tevye right when he said that we have a mighty God?..

So that is the end of section *Balak*. Now we'll go back to section *Lech-lecho*—"Get thee out!" This lesson was taught to me not long ago, and in real truth. No fine speeches or moralizations could help me this time. But this story I must tell you in detail, with all the particulars, as you like stories to be told.

It was in the days of Mendel Beiliss—at the time when Mendel Beiliss, our scapegoat, suffered the torments of the damned for someone else's sin, and the whole world was in a turmoil over the affair. One day I was sitting on the *prizba*, lost deep in thought. It was a hot summer day, the sun was baking my head as I meditated: But how, how could this be possible? In our times! Such a wise world! Such great people! And where is God! The ancient Jewish God? Why is He silent? How does He permit such a thing? How, and why, and wherefore!!! Such thoughts about God lead one to ponder over Heavenly things, to speculate: What is *this* world? What is the *next* one? And why doesn't the Messiah come? Eh, I said to myself, wouldn't he do a smart thing, the Messiah, if he came riding along on his white horse right now! Wouldn't that be a wonderful sight! It seems to me that our Jewish folk never needed him so badly as they do today! I don't know about the rich people, the Brodskys, for instance, in Yehupetz, or the Rothschilds in Paris. It may well be that they don't give a hoot for him; but we, the poor Jewish people of Dasrilovka and Mazepovka and Zlodeyevka, and even of Yehupetz, and even of Odessa, are looking forward to his coming. Oh, how we wait for him! Our eyes are practically popping out of our heads from the strain of watching out for his arrival! Our only hope now is that God will perform a miracle and the Messiah will come!..

Meanwhile, as I sat lost in such thoughts, I looked up and—a white horse was approaching, with a rider on its back. The man pulled up his horse right at my gate. Whoa! He got off, hitched the horse to a gatepost and came right up to me.

147

"*Zdravstvui,* Tevel!"*

"*Zdravstvuite, zdravstvuite, vashe blagorodiye,*"** I answered, quite warmly, while my heart said, *"Haman approacheth"*—you are looking forward to the Messiah so the *uryadnik,* the village policeman, arrives...

I stood up to greet him, the *uryadnik,* that is:

"Welcome, welcome, be my guest, what's new in the wide world and what good word will you say to me, Your Honor?" But my heart was almost springing out of my chest, so anxious was I to know what his business with me was. However he, the *uryadnik,* was in no hurry. He lit up a cigarette, blew out the smoke, spat, and then asked me:

"How much time, for instance, do you need, Tevel, in order to sell your house and all your belongings?"

I looked at him in amazement: "Why should I sell my house? In whose, for instance, way is it?" I asked.

"It's in nobody's way," said he, "but I've come to send you away from the village."

"Is that all, nothing else? For what good deeds? How did I come to earn such an honor?" I asked.

"It isn't I who am sending you away," he answered. "It's the *guberniya*—the provincial authorities."

"The *guberniya?*" I asked. "What has it noticed on me that it doesn't like?"

"It's not you alone," he said, "and not from here alone—from all the villages around, from Zlodeyevka, from Grabilovka, from Kostolomovka***, and even from Anatovka that was up till now a *shtetl* but has also become a village. All, all your people will be driven out."

"Even Leizer-Wolf the Butcher?" I asked. "And Naftole-Gershon the Lame, too? And the Anatovka *shokhet?* And the Rabbi?"

"All, all of them, everybody!" said he and even made a cutting gesture with his hand, as if he were holding a knife...

This made me feel a little better. As we say, *"The troubles of the many are a half-consolation."* However, I was greatly vexed by the

---

*"Hello, Tevye!" (Russian.)—*Tr.*

**"How do you do, Your Honor!" (Russian.)—*Tr.*

***The names of the villages are derived from the Russian words *zlodei*—villain, *grabitel*—burglar, and *kostolom*—bone-breaker.—*Ed.*

148

injustice of the thing, and an anger burned in me, so I said to him, to the *uryadnik:*

Tell me, do you at least know, *vashe blagorodiye,* Your Honor, that is, that I have lived in this village much longer than you? Do you know that my father, may he rest in peace, lived right here, in this corner, as did my grandfather, may he rest in peace, and my grandmother, may she rest in peace?" I counted out my whole family by their names, told him where they had lived and where they had died...

He heard me out all right, but when I finished talking he said:

"You're a funny Jew, Tevel, and you've got nine measures of speech in you. Of what good are your stories about your grandmother and grandfather? Let them enjoy their rest in Paradise. And you, Tevel," he went on, "you go pack your bag and baggage and clear out—march-march to Berdichev!"

This made me still angrier: wasn't it enough that he'd brought me such good tidings, this Esau, so he has to pile insult on injury, jeer at me—"march-march to Berdichev!" Let me at least give him a piece of my mind... So I said: "Your honor! In all the years since you became the Chief here, how many times did you hear any neighbor of mine complain that Tevye stole something, robbed him, cheated him, or just took something? You just ask among the householders whether we haven't always been on the friendliest terms? Haven't I come to you, Your Honor, many times to intercede for the peasants, begging you not to be so harsh with them?"

This, apparently, he didn't like! He got to his feet, crumpled his cigarette, threw it away, and said:

"I have no time to engage in idle chatter with you. I received a paper and the rest is none of my business! Here, sign this paper, you're given three days to sell off your belongings and get ready to leave."

I saw that things were bad and nothing could be done, but I said:

"You're giving me three days, that's what you're giving me? For that may you live three years in honor and in riches. May God repay you manifold for the good tidings you've brought me!"

I let him have it, as Tevye knows how! What's the difference, I thought, since I have to leave anyhow. What is there to lose? But had I been at least twenty years younger, and had my Golda, may she rest in peace, been alive, and if I were the same Tevye the Dairyman as in olden times I would have fought until blood flowed! But now? *"What are we and what is our life?"* What am I today and who am I? Only half the man I used to be, a splinter, a broken vessel!

Oh, Lord of the Universe, God Almighty! I thought to myself. Why do You always pick on Tevye? Why don't You sometimes play a game—just for fun—with, say, a Brodsky or a Rothschild? Why aren't they taught the lesson *Lech-lecho*—"Get thee out!"? It would be more to the point with them than with me. First of all, they would get the real taste of what it means to be a Jew. Secondly, let them, too, feel that we have a mighty God....

Oh, well, this is all empty talk. With God you don't argue, and you don't give Him advice on how to run the world. When He said: *"Mine is the Heaven and mine is the Earth,"* it means that He is the Master and we must obey Him. Whatever He says is said!

I went into the house and told my widowed daughter the good news:

"Tzeitl, we are moving out of this village, someplace to a town. We've lived in a village long enough," I said. "*'He who changes his place changes his luck....'* Go and start packing the bedding and bedclothes, the samovar and all the rest of our junk, while I go out to sell the house. A paper has arrived which orders us to clear out of here in three days. Three days from now, not even a whiff of us must remain here!"

These tidings made my daughter burst into tears, and looking at her, her little children, for no reason at all, also began to cry. Our house was full of wailing and laments as if it were *Tishab b'Ab,* the day on which we mourn the destruction of the Temple! This made me good and angry, and I poured the bitterness of my heart out on my poor daughter:

"What do you want from my life?! What's all this blubbering for all of a sudden? Like an old cantor at the first prayer on a fast-day?.. What am I—God's favorite son? Am I the only one to be so honored? Aren't plenty of Jews being driven out of the villages now? You should have heard what the *uryadnik* said! Even your Anatovka that was a *shtetl* up to now has, with God's help, also become a village—probably on account of the Anatovka Jews, so that all of them could be driven out. If that's how it is, then how am I worse than all the other Jews?"

In this manner I tried to comfort her, my daughter, that is. But being a woman, she said:

"Where will we go to, so suddenly? Where will we go to look for towns?"

150

"Fool!" said I. "When God came to our great-great-grandfather, our Ancestor Abraham, and said to him 'Lech-lecho'—'Get thee out of thy country!'—did Abraham question Him then, did he ask: 'Where shall I go?' God told him: *'Go unto the land which I will show thee'*—which simply means 'to all the four corners of the world...' We'll go," I said, "wherever our eyes lead us, wherever all the Jews go! Whatever happens to the Children of Israel will happen to Reb Israel. Are you a greater aristocrat than your sister Beilke who was a millionairess? If it suits her now to be with her Padhatzur in America and 'make a living' there, then what we'll have here is good enough for you... Thank the Lord that we at least have the means to move. A little is still left over from before, the cattle and chattels we sold also brought us something, and something will come in from the sale of the house. From a speck and a speck you get a full peck—and *'that too is for the best'!* But even if, God forbid, we had nothing," I said, "we'd still be better off than Mendel Beiliss!"

In a word, I managed to persuade her not to be so obstinate. I made it clear that when an *uryadnik* comes and brings a paper saying you must go you can't be a swine and you have to go. After that I went out into the village to fix up the matter of the house. I went directly to Ivan Poperilo, the *starosta*, the elder, that is, of the village. He was a well-to-do man and had long had his eye on my house. I went into no explanations—I'm no fool—I simply said:

"I want you to know, my dear Ivan, that I'm forsaking you."

"Why so?" he asked.

"I'm moving into a *shtetl*. I want to live among Jews. I'm no longer young. What if, God forbid, I should go and die?.."

"Why can't you die right here? Who is preventing you?"

I thanked him kindly and said: "You'd better do the dying here yourself, you'll find it more handy, while I'd rather go and die among my own people... But my house, Ivan, my house and kitchen garden. To another person I wouldn't sell, only to you."

"How much do you want for your house?"

"How much will you give me?"

"How much," he repeated, "do you want for it?"

Again I asked how much he was willing to pay. So we haggled and bargained and slapped each other's hands until at last we came to terms. I took a good down payment so that he shouldn't, God forbid, change his mind—I was too smart for him. And that was how I sold off in one day—dirt-cheap, of course—my whole property, turned everything into money, and then went to hire a wagon to cart off the remaining odds and ends of poverty.

But what happened after that—only to Tevye do such things happen! Listen attentively, I won't keep you long, I'll tell it to you in two, as they say, words.

Just before it was time to leave, I entered the house. It was no longer a home, it was a ruin. Bare walls that literally shed tears! The floor was strewn with bundles, bundles, and bundles! On the stove sat the cat, a poor, orphaned creature—it looked so mournful, it cut me to the heart and brought tears to my eyes...If I weren't ashamed of showing such weakness before my daughter I would have had me a good cry. After all, as one says, my father's house!.. Here I grew up, this is where I struggled and suffered all my days, and now, suddenly—*Lech-lecho!* Say what you will, it is a sorrowful thing!

But Tevye is not a woman, so I restrained myself and pretended to be in a cheerful mood. I called out to my daughter the widow: "Come here, Tzeitl," I said, "where are you?"

She came out from the other room, her eyes red and her nose swollen. Aha, I said to myself, my daughter has started her lamentations again, like an old woman on the Day of Atonement! These women, I tell you, the least excuse and they cry! Tears come cheap with them.

"Fool!" I said to her. "What are you crying for again? Aren't you silly? Just think of the difference between you and Mendel Beiliss."

But she paid no attention to my words and said:

"*Tateh,* you don't know why I am crying."

"I know the reason very well, why shouldn't I know it? You are crying," said I, "because it grieves you to leave your home. Here you were born, here you grew up, so it hurts you to part from it!.. Believe me, if I weren't Tevye, if I were someone else, I would kiss these bare walls and these empty shelves... I would drop down to this ground!.. I am just as sorry as you are for every last bit! Foolish child! Even this cat—do you see how it sits there on the stove like a poor orphan? A mute tongue, an animal, and yet—what a pity, it is being left behind all alone without a master, *tsar-balekhaim*—a pity for living things..."

"There is someone else who is still more to be pitied," said Tzeitl.

"Namely?"

"Namely," she said, "we are going away and leaving one person here, lonely as a stone."

I couldn't understand what she meant. "What are you babbling about? Where's the fire? What person? What stone?" I asked.

"*Tateh,*" she answered, "I am speaking about our Chava."

When she said these words I felt, I swear, as if I'd been scalded with boiling water or clubbed over the head! My anger aroused, I began to shout:

"Why all of a sudden Chava?! How many times have I told you that Chava was never to be mentioned or remembered!"

Do you think this scared her? Tevye's daughters have a power in them!

"*Tateh,*" she said, "don't get so angry, better remember what you yourself have said many times. You said that it stands written that a human being must have compassion for another human being, as a father has compassion for his child."

How do you like that? Her words exasperated me still more, and I cried:

"You're speaking of compassion? Where was *her* compassion when I cringed like a dog before the priest, his name should be blotted out, when I kissed his feet while she was probably in the next room and heard every word?.. Or where was her compassion when her mother, may she rest in peace, was lying—this shouldn't happen to you—right here on the floor covered with a black cloth? Where was she then? And what about the nights when I couldn't sleep? And the heartache I suffered all the time and still suffer when I remember what she did to me, for whom she exchanged us—where was her pity for me?" I couldn't talk any more, my heart was pounding so...

Perhaps you think that Tevye's daughter found no words to answer me with?

"You yourself, *Tateh,* say that even God Himself forgives those who repent."

"Repentance?" I cried. "Too late! The twig that has once torn itself away from the tree must wither! The leaf that falls must rot, and don't you dare speak to me of this any more— '*Up to here and no further!*'"

In short, when Tzeitl saw that words availed her nothing— Tevye is not a person who can be won over with words—she fell on my neck, began to kiss my hands and cry:

"*Tateh,* may evil befall me, may I die right here on the spot if

153

"Our exile is her exile…Look, Tateh, here is her bundle!"

you repulse her as you did that time in the woods when she stretched out her hands to you and you turned your horse in the other direction and fled!"

"Why are you heckling me so?! What a nuisance, what a misfortune on my head!"

But she wouldn't let go of me, she held me by the hands and went on protesting: "May evil befall me, may I drop dead if you don't forgive her, she is your daughter just the same as I am!"

"What do you want from my life!" I cried. "She is no longer my daughter! She died a long time ago!"

"No," said Tzeitl, "she never died and she is again your daughter as before, because from the very first minute she learned that we were being sent out she told herself that we were *all* being sent out—she, too. Wherever we went—Chava herself told me this—she would also go. Our exile is her exile... Look, *Tateh*, here is her bundle!"

All this my daughter Tzeitl said in one breath, as we recite the names of Haman's ten sons in the *Megilah*, she didn't let me put in a word. She pointed to a bundle tied up in a red shawl, and immediately opened the door to the other room and called: "Chava!"

That is how it was, as I live...

So what shall I tell you, dear friend? She, Chava, just as they write in the story-books, appeared in the doorway, healthy, strong, and as beautiful as before. Hadn't changed the slightest bit, only there was a worried look on her face and her eyes were a little clouded. She held her head up proudly and looked at me—and I at her. Then she stretched out both hands to me, and could utter only one single word, almost in a whisper:

"*Ta-teh...*"

Please forgive me, but when I remember that day tears come to my eyes. But you shouldn't think that Tevye, God forbid, dropped a tear, or showed that he had a soft heart—nonsense! That is, what I then felt deep in my heart—that's something else. You yourself are also a father of children and you know as well as I do the meaning of the words, *"A father hath mercy on his children."* When a child, however it may have sinned, looks right into your heart and soul, and says *"Tateh!"*—come on, just try and drive it away!.. But on the other hand, I recalled the fine trick she had played on me... Fedka Galagan, damn him... and the priest, may his name be forgotten... and my tears... and Golda, may she rest in peace, stretched out on the floor, dead... Oh, no! Tell me yourself, how can one forget, how can one forget such things?.. But on the other hand again... how is it possible! After all, she was my child. *"A father hath mercy on his children."* How can a man be so cruel when God says of Himself that he is a *"long-suffering God and slow to anger..."* Especially since she had repented and wanted to return to her father and to her God!..

What have you to say to this, Mr. Sholom Aleichem? You are, after all, a man who writes books and you give the world advice, so tell me, what should Tevye have done? Should he have embraced her and kissed her, and said to her, as we say on Yom Kippur at Kol Nidre: *"I have forgiven thee in accordance with thy prayers"*—come to me, you are my child? Or perhaps I should have turned the shafts, as I did that time in the woods, and said to her: *"Lech-lecho"*—begone, that is, go back in good health to wherever you've come from?.. No, suppose you were in Tevye's place, tell me frankly, as between good friends, what would you have done? If you cannot answer me at once I'll give you time to think it over... Meanwhile, I must go— my grandchildren are already waiting for me, looking out for their grandfather. You must know that grandchildren are a thousand times more precious than children. *"Children and children's children"*—no small matter!

Please forgive me if I have given you a headache with my talk; at least, you'll have something to write about... And now—goodbye. If God wills it we shall probably meet again some day.

1914

[*Yekhalaklakoys*—"Slippery Places"—is a very short story previously never translated from the Yiddish,* written in 1916, just before that author's death, as an addition to "Get Thee Out!" In it Tevye, meeting the author by chance in a train, elaborates on how he managed to avert the lesson *Balak*—Vengeance—when the peasants came to beat him up or burn down his house. He told them that if they were in the right they would be able to repeat God's own words, hence the story might be called "Tongue-twisters." The following is the last paragraph of the story.]

---

*Our translator, Miriam Katz, apparently overlooked Curt Leviani's translation of this story as "Tevye Reads the Psalms" in Old Country Tales (1966)—The editors.

156

I have become a wanderer, one day here, another there. Ever since the lesson *Lekh-lekho* was read to me I have been on the move and know no place of rest where I could say, "Here, Tevye, is where you shall remain." Tevye asks no questions—he is told to go, he goes... Today, Mr. Sholom Aleichem, we meet in a train, tomorrow we may find ourselves in Yehupetz, next year—in Odessa, Warsaw, or even America—unless the Almighty looks around and says: "You know what, children? I'll send you down the Messiah!" Oh, how I wish He would play such a trick on us, He, the Ancient Lord of the Universe! And now—farewell. I wish you a happy journey, give my regards to all our people, and tell them not to worry: *Our ancient God still lives!*

1914—1916

157

AFTERWORD: And so ends our journey to meet Tevye, his family, and his world.

This special edition of *Tevye the Dairyman* has been set in larger types for ease of reading for both junior citizens and senior citizens. Manuel Bennett, the illustrator, has brought his talent and his Jewish childhood memories to create these inventive views of Sholem-Aleykhem's *Tevye* stories. If you wish to add any color into his sketches, as he enjoys doing himself from time to time, be free to do so, since the drawings lend themselves to color improvisations.

We are also grateful to Miriam Katz, who has allowed us to reproduce her translation of this edition of *Tevye the Dairyman.*

THE EDITORS